# BITTER
# RECOIL

## STEVEN F. HAVILL

# WORLDWIDE®

TORONTO • NEW YORK • LONDON
AMSTERDAM • PARIS • SYDNEY • HAMBURG
STOCKHOLM • ATHENS • TOKYO • MILAN
MADRID • WARSAW • BUDAPEST • AUCKLAND

For Kathleen

Recycling programs
for this product may
not exist in your area.

**Bitter Recoil**

A Worldwide Mystery/April 2015

First published by Poisoned Pen Press

ISBN-13: 978-0-373-26938-9

Copyright © 1992 by Steven F. Havill

**Printed in U.S.A.**

# Acknowledgments

I am grateful to several people for providing technical information that I used in this novel. I would like to thank in particular Fidel Duenas, Rick Jones and Paul Pierce.

# ONE

I STOPPED AT the top of the saddleback and looked down through the pines. The campgrounds were still a mile below me, hidden behind the fat swell of Steamboat Rock. I took a deep breath, found a big granite boulder, and sat down. This walking was worse medicine than pills or needles.

Walk, the damn doctors had said. Walk. I hated walking. That's what cars are for. Or elevators.

Nevertheless, the heart surgeon had convinced me that if I walked, gave up smoking, and shed my considerable girth, I might live a couple more years. I fumbled in my shirt pocket and pulled out a cigarette. Hell, I was walking. That was one out of three.

From where I sat, I could see all the way down Isidro Valley. The sky was a blank, merciless blue, and the sun beat down on my back, roasting right through my shirt. It burned out the kinks.

I had walked up a trail from the Steamboat Rock campground and had worked my way through the thick ponderosa pines for almost two miles. At first, the notion of a hike had seemed like a pleasant idea.... I had a long afternoon to kill before I tried cooking supper over the little gas grill stowed in the back of my Blazer.

After the first ten minutes, the hike had been nothing but sweaty, grinding work. And the Smokey Bear signs down along the highway hadn't been joking. The mountain was dry. The needles under my feet crackled like little shards of glass, and I probably shouldn't have even thought about a cigarette. I lit one and relaxed on the rock.

It was peaceful. Maybe wilderness hikers had something. Get away from it all; leave worries behind. I'd been working up a sweat and hadn't thought about Posadas County for nearly half an hour.

Here I was, basking in the sun like a fat toad, 300 miles north of my own New Mexico border town. For two hours I hadn't thought of the past winter, when I'd spent the valuable hours of my life dealing with an unpleasant and mixed bag of drunks, punks, child abusers, drug runners…or even simple, wacko souls like Vinnie Jaramillo, who'd arrived home one night in May to find his wife cheating on him. He'd taken a shotgun to his wife and her boyfriend while his three small children watched. Then he'd called the sheriff's department.

I hadn't gotten there first, but it wouldn't have mattered anyway. He'd waited until the first deputy arrived, and then, when he was sure he had an official witness, Vinnie sat down on the living room sofa and blew his own skull to pieces. It had been a hell of a mess.

I guess we were lucky Vinnie had kept his targets within the walls of his own home. And that's how it happened in Posadas County most of the time. Someone went off the deep end and made news. Maybe there's a natural tendency to think one's own community isn't as nuts as the rest of the world, where the loonies try to change the lives of complete strangers.

Hell, I still had a two-week-old copy of the Albuquerque newspaper tucked in my Blazer with headlines about the assassination of Washington State's governor, along with a Department of Corrections warden. According to the article, the governor had been fishing by himself, sitting peacefully in a canoe on some remote Washington lake, and a high-powered rifle bullet fired from hundreds of yards away had exploded his skull. And the prison warden had been shot later that same day when he stepped out of his station wagon to unlock the garage door of his suburban Tacoma home.

Real freaks running loose…the paper said the resulting manhunt was the largest Washington had ever had. We'd even gotten a teletype from Washington in our office, for God's sakes…probably because we sat right on the border with Mexico.

I took another drag on the cigarette and wished that I could keep my mind off work for more than a few seconds at a time. But replay, replay.

In Vinnie Jaramillo's case, for months afterward the scene still flogged my brain, unwanted but tenacious. The faces of the children left behind were the worst.

What do you do with a three-, four-, and six-year-old who've seen their parents splattered all over the wallpaper? The deputy and I had made some awkward motions and then with relief had watched my chief detective, Estelle Reyes, take the three traumatized and orphaned children under her wing.

She didn't try to stop their sobs, didn't try to distract them. Instead, she was just there, hugging them all close and giving them a spot safe from all the strangers. Later, she wouldn't let the relatives take the children until she was convinced the children understood what was happening to them.

I watched her teach the children, including the youngest one, her telephone number, the four of them playing with the telephone like it was one of those Kmart toys for tots. What a wonderful mind for law enforcement that woman had developed. And two weeks after that incident, her letter of resignation was on my desk, and I was plunged into the deepest funk I'd wallowed in for years.

I sighed. I admit it. I missed her damn near as much as I missed my own daughters. As undersheriff of Posadas County, I'd watched Estelle Reyes work for six years, moving from dispatcher to road patrol to detective—our only detective.

She'd come to us as a part-timer, a college student who showed a flair for common sense and organization. Stunning-looking, too. I know the lawyers who make their living from discrimination cases would be after me for saying so, but she brightened up our drab little office just with her presence. She'd even won the confidence of our sheriff, who viewed anything in skirts as either a sex object or a nuisance.

Shortly after the Jaramillo tragedy, she married a young physician, he as handsome as she was lovely. It was a hell of a wedding, and the department attended in full force…and we behaved ourselves throughout. The young couple's plans meshed nicely. Dr. Francis Guzman took a residency with the Public Health Service, running a clinic in San Estevan, 300 miles north of Posadas County and 6 miles down-canyon from where I now sat. Estelle had applied for a job with that county sheriff's department, and Sheriff Pat Tate had jumped at the chance.

His turf was a long, narrow county that was awkward to administer from the county seat far to the southeast, a county that was split down the center by a single state highway, with the rest dirt roads. Towns and villages were scattered far and wide. An Indian pueblo in the north end of the county made jurisdictional matters there even more interesting, especially since the pueblo had only a couple of law officers of its own.

Tate had had the good sense to assign Estelle to what he euphemistically called the San Estevan substation so she could avoid the forty-mile daily commute from the county seat to her new home. The "substation" turned out to be nothing more than a spare room in the highway department's district headquarters.

When I decided to take a short vacation late that summer—an escape from doctors who wouldn't mind their own business—I found myself traveling north. I didn't mean to pry, mind you, but I wanted to cruise through another county and see what Estelle Reyes-Guzman had won for herself. And if I had to walk, it might as well be in spectacular mountains that should be cooler than the summer blast furnace of Posadas.

I crushed out the cigarette and tucked the remains in my shirt pocket. I lay back on the rock with a groan of aching muscles, hat over my eyes. I had a dinner invitation from Estelle and Francis for Saturday…I hadn't told them I was coming up the day before. That gave me a good stretch to loaf and play outdoorsman. I knew me pretty well and twenty-four hours was about my limit for recreation. I even had grand plans to sleep in my Blazer, figuring if I parked clear in the back of the Steamboat Rock campground, I'd have peace and quiet.

The granite wasn't comfortable for long and I sat up.

Another hour would see me down to the campground, if I didn't take the short side trail out to the promontory of Steamboat Rock. I'd briefly imagined that I might walk up there, come the cool of the evening. Briefly.

I was sixty-two and fat, fully recovered from a quadruple bypass the winter before, but inclined to lie down and rest whenever someone mentioned serious exercise. I would do well to stumble my way back down to the campground, much less anything more strenuous. Even the grilled dinner was improbable. I knew damn well that when the time came, I'd settle for a couple of pieces of bologna on a hamburger bun, washed down with a beer or two.

And that's exactly what happened. I made it off the mountain without falling on my face or even having another cigarette. The last hundred yards were easiest, following a well-packed trail with no grade.

Back at the campground I unlocked the Blazer, stowed my daypack, and popped a beer. The sun was already filtering through the trees, ready to drop behind the rugged mesa rim. I unfolded an aluminum lounge chair and settled back to watch the mountain colors fade and blend.

The campground was quiet for a Friday night…for about five minutes. Then a big Winnebago pulled in, one of those things with the canvas awning that folds down from one tall, slab side. Two elderly folks made home away from home in that monster…all thirty feet of it. In minutes they had a covered patio with a gas-fired barbecue grill sending up plumes of cooking chicken.

Two slots down was a Volkswagen bus, crammed to the gills with two young couples and an endless supply of noisy, scrapping children. They should have hijacked the Winnebago and had some room. Another Blazer, a couple years newer than mine, pulled in, and the first creature to emerge was a Dalmatian, nose to the ground and on a beeline for my peaceful corner. He snuffled up, tail wagging, expecting me to pat his wide, empty head.

"Get out of here, brute," I said and waved a hand.

"Pokie, come!" his owner called and Pokie angled off to bother someone else. I opened another beer, just about ready to start sulking. Hell, I could have parked just as easily in a convenience store lot and had more privacy. I needed to find a rough old Forest Service road leading out to nowhere so I could vegetate in peace.

I scowled and looked across the large campground toward the highway. Several of the children from the Volkswagen were barefoot, and I wondered if their parents realized how much broken glass littered the place.

"Jesus, Gastner," I muttered aloud. How the hell had I gotten so adept at minding other people's business? Occupational hazard, I guess. By 8:30 I stopped fighting the fatigue that kept me from making any effort to move to a more secluded spot. I crawled into the back of the Blazer where the mattress was soft and cool. With windows cracked for air I was asleep in half a minute, despite the shrieks of playing children and the endless slamming of car doors.

And it seemed no more than half a minute before the first siren jerked me awake in the deep pitch of that mountain night.

# TWO

I SAT UPRIGHT in the Blazer and cracked my head on the roll-bar brace. I cursed and flopped back down, one hand clamped to my skull and the other scrabbling for my glasses.

The siren that had awakened me was just down-canyon, coming hard up the winding mountain highway. I heard the vehicle enter the sweeping curve just before the turnoff to the campground. The tires squawled on the pavement. The engine bellowed and then the car was past us.

I sat up more carefully this time and could see the red lights winking through the thick timber. Almost immediately the emergency vehicle slowed. They had reached the call, whatever it was. At the same time, far in the distance, another siren note floated up from the valley below.

After some more searching I found my flashlight and looked at my watch. I was surprised to see 3:18.

If there had been a collision, I hadn't heard it. I snapped off the light and peered outside. No one else in the campground was stirring. Maybe someone had sailed their car off into the canyon…the road was ripe for it at any of dozens of places. If they had, they'd done it quietly since I hadn't heard a thing.

I lay back down, listening as the second siren note pulsed and wailed. I didn't have this county's frequency on my radio, or my curiosity would have been easily satisfied.

But hell, it wasn't any of my business. I had an invitation for dinner in another fifteen hours, and over the frijoles Estelle Reyes-Guzman could tell me all about whatever had happened. Maybe it was the state cops anyway.

"The hell with it," I muttered and threw my sleeping bag open. I was wide awake now and would remain so. My biological clock didn't take much monkeying with to be screwed up completely. In country like this somebody might need a hand.

I pulled on my boots, buttoned my shirt, and ran a hand through my hair before pulling on my cap. That would have to do. Mindful of the damn roll bar, I climbed into the driver's seat of the Blazer, fumbled the keys, and started the vehicle. The fat tires crunched gravel as I backed out. I didn't turn on the headlights until I reached the bridge across the creek, ready to climb the upgrade to the highway.

An ambulance roared around the corner of the state highway, and I waited until he'd shot past before I pulled out to follow northbound. The highway jogged left around a buttress of jutting rock, then eased along the river gorge with only a set of stubby guardrails keeping vehicles from zinging off into the void.

In another quarter of a mile I was greeted by a psychedelic display of colored lights bouncing off rocks, trees, and the tight walls of the canyon. A county sheriff's car was pulled diagonally across the highway, blocking my northbound lane. The ambulance had pulled around that car and parked on up ahead, blocking the lane from the other direction.

I slowed to a crawl, obeying the flashlight signals of a man standing near the highway's center yellow lines. Behind him, parked on the southbound lane's shoulder and snugged right up against the rocks that formed the near-vertical embankment, was a dark-colored pickup. My headlights reflected off the white front license plate, and I guessed Forest Service even before the man stepped up to my Blazer.

I rolled down the window, held up my badge, and said, "I'll park up ahead, behind the ambulance."

The young man frowned and rested a hand on the door of my Blazer as if he were going to hold it in place with five fingers. I knew exactly what he was thinking. There were at least a million ambulance chasers in the country, many of them with Special Deputy commissions and pot-metal badges. They showed up like the goon squads at every serious accident or fire, making pests of themselves.

I held the wallet still until he'd focused the flashlight on it and read enough to be satisfied. "That would be fine, sir," he said. "And we sure need someone up at the other end, catching cars coming down that way. There's just a civilian up there."

"You got it." I drove around the patrol car, avoided the orange cones that straddled the centerline, swung past the ambulance, and parked in the center of the highway. I turned on the red grill lights. Their light pulsed on the anxious face of a middle-aged man who walked toward me from up the road. A Buick was pulled off on the shoulder fifty yards ahead. I took my red-head flashlight from the glove compartment and climbed out.

"Use this," I said and handed the man the red light.

"There's not going to be much traffic this time of night, but if there is, we want 'em at a crawl. I'll be back to give you a hand in just a minute."

"Oh. Okay," he said, then hesitated. He looked at the light as if it were about to bite him.

"Just wave 'em down. Another officer will probably be here in a minute or two anyway."

I walked back down the highway, past the ambulance. The harsh spotlights from the patrol car converged on a spot near the guardrails where the ambulance attendants and the officer worked over a single figure crumpled on the ground. The victim was lying facedown. I could see one leg extended under the guardrail.

"Let's immobilize her just the way she is," one of the attendants said. "I think we can do that."

I kept out of the way. I don't think the emergency crew even knew I was there. I recognized the deputy sheriff even in the tricky light of the spots and flashlights. But it was no time for a reunion with Estelle Reyes-Guzman.

I took the opportunity to step to the rail and beam my own flashlight down into the rocks. There was no vehicle in sight. Maybe the victim had been a pedestrian, maybe drunk. They had said "she." Maybe she'd staggered into the path of a car and been clipped. If so, it had to have been hit-and-run. If the man up the road with the Buick had been involved, they sure as hell wouldn't have left him up there by himself, directing traffic.

I turned away from the rail and took a closer look. The victim was female and appeared to be young, perhaps in her twenties. I didn't have much of a view but she looked vaguely familiar to me.

The attendants transferred her to the gurney with a minimum of movement, and I could see from the extent of their emergency field dressings that she was hurt in a dozen places. One leg was bent near the hip at an impossible angle.

With a coordinated effort the two paramedics picked up the gurney and carried the victim to the ambulance. I felt a hand on my arm and turned.

"You're just in time," Estelle Reyes-Guzman said. "I saw you drive up."

Miss Sharp Eyes hadn't missed me after all. "Yeah," I said. "I was camping out and you woke me up. What have you got here?"

"I don't know."

"Pedestrian?"

Estelle played her flashlight over the area where the victim's body had been. "Let me show you." We walked to the guardrail. "We have a single victim, as far as we can tell right now. Haven't found anyone else. The gentleman who owns the Buick up where you parked saw her first and used his CB radio. The owner of the all-night convenience store up at the head of the canyon heard him and called me. She was lying right here when I arrived. Les Cook with the Forest Service had stopped before I got here. He's over there working traffic. He said the same thing. She was lying here, part under the rail."

"Sounds like she got hit pretty hard," I said. "A little more and she'd have been down in the rocks and probably wouldn't have been found for days."

"I think that's where she was," Estelle said. "Look

here." She motioned for me to bend over the steel guardrail. "Don't step over yet, though," she added as she saw me make a move to do just that. "See right here?" She pointed and held the light close. On the back flange of the rail were bloody fingerprints. "I think she grabbed here to help pull herself up to the rail."

"Is there blood on the bottom of the flange?" I asked. "If she grabbed ahold, her thumbprint would be on the bottom."

Estelle crouched down low and ducked her head. The bottom of the rail was about eighteen inches off the ground, and she played the beam of the flashlight along the steel surface. "There's blood opposite," she said. "Look here."

"I'll take your word for it." If I had scrunched down in that position, I'd never have gotten up. I turned the light to shine on the slope. The rocky incline was just highway fill, and the scuff marks that might be made by someone crawling up the slope would be hard to see…especially by flashlight. Undaunted, Estelle stepped over the rail and examined the ground.

"Lots of blood," she said, and she worked her way carefully down the steep slope, keeping her own feet off to one side of the track she was following. "I think she crawled up here. See the dislodged rocks?"

"You need to look at it in daylight."

"I'll take a set of pictures now. Can I get you to hold the light so I can focus?"

"Of course." I knew Estelle's affinity for photography. When she worked for my county, our film-processing bill had been astronomical. But her results were equally so.

Before she went to work, we made the highway a

little safer. I walked south and stabbed a flare in the centerline, and then we repositioned the cones, Estelle's county car, and my Blazer. After taking down what information we needed from the man in the Buick, we let him go. He didn't waste any time. The timber cop agreed to stay for a while and manage traffic…I think two cars had gone by since I had arrived.

Estelle set up her 35mm camera and took a series of photos of the slope, each picture downhill from the last, while I held the flashlight so she could focus. The electronic flash was like a lightning bolt in the narrow canyon.

When she was satisfied, she said, "We can take a close look come dawn, but this way, if it rains or something, we're covered a little. Look here."

I did and could see that the blood trail turned at the base of the steepest part of the embankment and then angled away to the south.

"The way she was broken up, moving that far took some set of nerves," I said.

Estelle took more pictures. Together we followed the trail. The girl had crawled, apparently pulling herself forward with only her hands and sheer will, for fifty yards along the base of the embankment before trying to climb it. The trail led back through a thick stand of grass, and we saw the crushed stems left by the girl's passing. The grass gave way to a jumble of boulders, and a smear of blood on one of them showed us where the girl had slid off the rock into the grass.

"Christ," I said. Estelle muttered something and reloaded her camera. She started up on the rocks, and I said quickly, "Watch for the goddamned snakes." She ignored the warning.

"I think this is it," Estelle said.

"'It' what?"

Estelle played the flashlight on the rocks. From where she stood, the highway embankment up to the guardrails was a seventy- or eighty-degree slope. "The blood ends here," she said. "At least I can't see any more."

"Nothing coming down from the roadway?"

"Not that I can see. Shine your light right up here." She indicated the slope. I did so, and she snapped more pictures. "I don't see any scuff marks," she added and then climbed down to where I stood. "I want to climb up the embankment over there, where we won't be apt to obliterate anything. Maybe there are marks up by the highway."

We made the climb, with me huffing and puffing. There were no marks on the highway shoulder, nothing on the steel rail. The only marks on the highway's road surface itself were two short skid marks, about twenty yards south of where Estelle's patrol car was parked. The marks were straight and centered in the lane, as if someone had spiked the brakes without swerving. The marks were short—the vehicle hadn't been traveling fast.

"They might not even be related," I said.

"And probably aren't," Estelle said. She took pictures anyway.

"So what do you think?" I asked as she put the camera gear back in the trunk of her car.

"I just don't know, sir. I really don't. It looks like she was struck and knocked over the rail back there, maybe hit so hard she flew over it, and landed on the rocks. Then she crawled to where we found her. That's all I can imagine." She frowned.

"Maybe," I said. "But if someone gets nailed by a car hard enough to toss 'em down a goddamned cliff onto rocks, I can't believe they'd survive, much less be able to crawl so far."

"That's what bothers me," Estelle said. "Maybe we'll be able to piece something together when we have the medical report."

"She didn't have any identification?"

"None."

"Terrific." I looked at my watch. It was already quarter of five. "What now?"

"I want to walk down along the road and see if I come up with anything. And then up the other way. By then it'll be dawn and we can see what we missed."

"What do you want me to do?"

"You're on vacation, sir."

"Pretend I'm not. I had a couple hours of vacation yesterday. That was probably enough."

Estelle smiled and shook her head. "Maybe you'd go down to San Estevan, where they took the girl. She'll go to the clinic there first and no doubt be transferred to Albuquerque. You might be able to find something out there."

I nodded. "Invitation for dinner still on for tonight?"

"Of course." She slammed the trunk closed. "By then this'll be all wrapped up."

Estelle Reyes-Guzman wasn't wrong too often.

# THREE

By the time I reached the public health clinic in San Estevan, the victim had been airlifted to Albuquerque. The EMTs in the ambulance had been quick-witted and efficient. They knew that the extent of the girl's injuries was more than the clinic could handle. The helicopter air ambulance, a Bell Jet Ranger, had been dispatched from the city and made the roundtrip flight before I left the mountain.

As I drove into the village at six in the morning, San Estevan was beginning the rooster and barking dog stage of awakening. I drove past the Catholic retreat complex north of the village and caught sight of one friar or monk or whatever he was, as he crossed from one white adobe building to another, toiletry kit in hand.

A hundred yards beyond and on the opposite side of the road was a National Park Service historic site, the restoration of Gualate Ruin, a two-story stone structure that I'd heard was one of the dozens of outliers for the major ruin at Chaco Canyon to the west.

None of the feds were up yet, nor was there life stirring at the Forest Service District Office, a low, flat building tucked in the cottonwoods where the state highway turned away from the river and into the village.

No more than two dozen houses, scattered here

and there across the narrow valley, made up the ancient village of San Estevan. Originally, the town had sprung up on the edge of the Indian pueblo, a mixture of clergy, traders, and farmers.

A few of the houses were massive, with adobe walls a yard thick and large courtyards—architecture that said there'd been some rich times in the valley.

But the inevitable was happening. The village was just outside the pueblo's reservation, and so the valley was salted now with crackerbox shacks and trailers, bright aluminum mobile homes insulting the stolid, ancient adobes as city folk established their weekend camps and "ranchettes," as the Realtors say.

If I drove a thousand yards south of the village's gas station, south of the modern clutter and detritus of seasonal residents, I could imagine that a century had been peeled away.

The pueblo, one of the state's smallest, was neat and uniformly reddish-brown. Burnt sienna adobes with mud ovens in every yard, neat stacks of piñon and juniper firewood behind every dwelling, narrow brown lanes packed hard as cement between the houses, all leading down to the brown-trunked cottonwoods that screened the river from view.

The demarcation between pueblo land and private land beginning with the village of San Estevan was as obvious as if there were a solid wall between the two.

I passed the Texaco station and, where the highway jogged another right angle turn, the combination of Dairy Queen and general store. Just beyond, a group of three trailers was parked willy-nilly to form a compound filled with wrecked car and truck carcasses, and beyond those was a fenced pasture where two horses grazed themselves fat.

Remembering Estelle's directions, I looked for the sign and found it nearly camouflaged by purple bee-weed. Below the sign for the San Estevan Clinic, United States Public Health Service, an arrow pointed to a graveled lane.

I pulled into the clinic's driveway and parked beside a blue Isuzu Trooper with Posadas County plates. No matter where they moved in the state, Estelle and Francis Guzman would carry that tag until it rusted to pieces...a gentle reminder of their home to the south.

Only one other vehicle was in the lot, an older model GMC pickup—maybe a '55 or '56. It was no collector's item, though, just an aging, battered work truck.

I crushed out my cigarette and walked inside the building. The clinic was cramped, with a twelve-by-twelve waiting room, a tiny cell for the receptionist, and a narrow hallway that led back to the treatment rooms. I guessed there were two of those at the most. I heard a metal pan clatter and voices, and then an Indian woman stuck her head out of one of the examining room doors. She saw me and held up a hand with one finger raised.

"I'll be right out," she said and disappeared again. I turned, looked around the waiting room, and saw universal doctor's office decorations...aging magazines, a few children's books. A large Ojo de Dios woven out of gaudy yarn hung on one wall and a sand painting of an Indian dancer in an awkward pose on another.

Across the room on the west wall was a framed state map with a large water stain rumpling all of Colfax, Mora, San Miguel, and Guadalupe counties. Beside the map was a framed aerial photograph of a mountain in fall colors, aspens aflame. It was no local mountain, of course...probably one from Colorado or Wyoming—wherever the postcard artist had been able to find a nice, conical, generic mountain with no towns, powerlines, or highways to mar the picture.

I stepped to the window and looked out at chamiso, cactus, and rocks.

"May I help you?"

I turned quickly. The nurse had a pencil and metal clipboard poised at the ready. She was older than I had first thought. Steel gray was beginning to temper her ebony hair, tied back tightly in a bun. Her black eyes regarded me calmly from a broad, flat face whose flawless skin was like burnished walnut. I read the name tag on her white blouse and wondered how long Mary Vallo had been an R.N. She might have been forty years old or sixty-five.

"Good morning, Mrs. Vallo," I said. "I'm Bill Gastner, undersheriff of Posadas County, down in the southern part of the state. I've been assisting Deputy Guzman with an accident investigation this morning." I started the standard smoker's fumble for a cigarette and thought better of it. "I wondered if I could talk with Dr. Guzman for a minute, if he's not tied up."

"Surely," Mary Vallo said. "Come on back." She led the way down the hall, and in one small cubbyhole I saw a coffeemaker just beginning to drip. Sharp-eyed Mary saw my glance and said, "I just started it. I'll get you a cup as soon as it's ready."

"Wonderful," I said, feeling about three hours overdue for my first morning caffeine buzz.

The examining room we entered was small and the

scene of considerable recent action. Mary Vallo resumed her labors, at that moment cleaning the spatters from the front of the portable X ray unit. Francis Guzman was sitting at a table by the window awash with paperwork. His white smock was white in small spots only. He glanced up, not eager to move.

"Well, I'll be damned!" the young physician exclaimed, and he pushed himself away from the table, extending a hand to me at the same time. "You're about the last person I expected to see at this hour. How have you been, Sheriff?"

"Just fine, except that wife of yours has been putting me to work." At his puzzled expression, I added, "The accident this morning with the girl pedestrian happened just above where I was camping. And you know the way old cops are. I couldn't help snooping."

"Up at Steamboat, you mean?"

"Yes. And how is the girl?"

Guzman shook his head and sat down again. He was six inches taller than my five-eight and built like an athlete, but now he looked like he'd just finished the pentathlon.

"I don't think she's going to make it, Sheriff. She has about eight broken bones, including her skull. She's hemorrhaging internally as well as suffering a dozen gashes and lacerations. She was out there a while, you know, before anybody found her. I was surprised she hadn't bled to death."

"And with all that, she still managed to crawl almost a hundred yards," I said and accepted a foam cup of coffee from Mary Vallo.

"You're kidding."

I shook my head. "The last few yards were up a

steep embankment, back up to the highway shoulder. It looked like after she was hit, she ended up on a pile of boulders down by the river. At that point the highway embankment is almost vertical. Since she couldn't crawl up there, she apparently moved in the only direction she could, along the stream in the grass until she reached a spot where she could try for the road again."

"I don't see how that would have been possible," Guzman said. "I really don't." He stood up. "Look at this." He had a set of small X rays and he handed the top one to me.

"We don't have very good equipment, but even so, look at that hip." He traced the fracture with his index finger.

Even I could see the damage. The head of the femur looked like it had been pried off the shaft, taking a chip of the hip socket with it.

"And her right arm was broken in three places. Her left ankle was snapped. There are what look like compressed fractures of two lower vertebrae. And a comminuted fracture of the right parietal."

"What's that?"

He tapped the side of his skull above his ear. "With all that and the bleeding, I can't believe she crawled."

"No one was there to help her that we know of," I said. "Not as far as we've been able to determine. Of course, it's hard to tell. But Estelle's still there and might turn up something."

Francis Guzman leaned forward, hands clasped and forearms resting on his knees. He remained silent, deep in thought. Finally he said, "The other thing that bothers me about her injuries—and I'm no great expert, you understand—what bothers me is that they're not really consistent with being smacked by a car or truck. I know that's what the ambulance attendants told me, but still..."

"Meaning?" I sat back, my chair leaning against the wall. I wanted a cigarette, but the "Thank You For Not Smoking" sign was staring me in the face.

"If a car hits you hard enough to do serious damage, to fling you right over a guardrail, there's usually some clue that that's what happened."

"Well, sure." I'd seen hundreds of accident victims in twenty years.

"But there were no paint chips, Sheriff. No chrome. Nothing."

I shrugged. "That happens all the time."

"Maybe. But there were no sharp lacerations, the sort of injury we'd expect from headlights and rims and bumpers or grill parts. And we'd see those in relationship with traumatic fractures and deep tissue bruising."

He paused, then added, "And look at the fractures. Her right hip, Sheriff. The sort of fracture you get in football, when the joint is yanked and wrenched the wrong way. No compression injuries related with the fracture, except minor scrapes. Now, the major lacerations on her broken right arm were contaminated with rocks and dirt. The same thing is true of her broken left ankle."

Guzman was warming up and I let him continue without interruption.

"And see here, on her skull. She took a hell of a rap there. You know what I found in her hair? Besides dirt? Lichen. The stuff that grows on rocks. Flakes of it right in the wound. Her head hit a rock, Sheriff, and hit it hard."

"Well, we know that. That's likely where the other fractures came from…or some of them. When she landed on the rocks. She was walking along the highway and got clipped. The impact threw her over the embankment. She tumbled ass over teakettle down into the rocks, breaking who knows what on the way."

Francis Guzman shook his head. "Where did the car hit her?" He stood up and pretended to be walking along the road. "Right hip? She turns and it's her left hip that's facing traffic, not right." I grimaced. The young doctor had a hell of an imagination.

"Come on, Francis. She could have just as easily turned the other way."

"Not likely. And that leg was yanked out of its socket, not impacted."

"So what are you saying happened?"

"I'm not sure, but I'm willing to bet she was never hit by a vehicle of any kind."

"What, then?"

Francis Guzman hesitated. "I think she was thrown over the embankment."

"Oh, you do."

He nodded. "The rest fits that way, too."

"The rest?"

"There was an attempt at rape, Sheriff. I'm sure of that. And what I'd say were deep fingernail gouges on her back, near the base of her neck. Her hands were busted up pretty badly, and I didn't have a chance to check under her fingernails. The M.E. in Albuquerque will do that. And it looks like she was punched hard in the mouth. Right here." He touched the left corner of his own mouth. "Not the sort of injury caused by sharp rocks. But a fist, yes." I toyed with my empty and crumpled coffee cup. "It's hard to believe the other injuries were caused by sliding down an embankment like that."

"Not if she were thrown from a moving vehicle it's not."

I stared at Guzman incredulously. "Tossed out of the back of a moving pickup truck, you mean? Something like that? Jesus. A hit-and-run I can imagine. But the other?"

Guzman nodded and glanced at his watch. "That's what I think. You've got at least one murder on your hands. I'd bet on it."

"She's not dead yet, Doc."

Guzman looked pained. "No, but her baby is. The young lady was four months pregnant."

# FOUR

I STARED AT Francis Guzman. He misunderstood my silence and said again, "She was pregnant. Lost the fetus, of course."

"I heard you," I murmured. "Did you know her? Was she from around here?"

"I think that she's been living in the village for about six months to a year." Guzman had gotten to his feet wearily, like a man a decade older than I. With a grunt, he opened the window beside the desk. The air that washed into the room was fresh and tinted with sage.

"Her name's Cecilia Burgess. She didn't have any identification on her when she was brought in last night, but both my nurse and I knew her. I met her about…well, four months ago. She came in for a prenatal checkup." Guzman stepped out of the room and then reappeared with the coffeepot. "More?"

"No, thanks. And then you saw her off and on after that?"

"That's right." He smiled but without much humor. "Estelle's got you drawn right into this mess, hasn't she?"

I realized I was grilling the doc as if he were a witness—which he probably would be sooner or later—and as if it were my own investigation, which it certainly wasn't. "Sorry," I said. "Occupational hazard."

"Can't help but be curious," Guzman said and sat

down, long legs stretched out in front of him. "There are a lot of answers I'd like, but I'm so damn tired I can't think straight." He grinned. "Estelle's going to bust in here in a few minutes and give me the third degree, so I might as well warm up with you, right?"

"Might as well. I can't help being a nosy old bastard. Who was the girl's husband?"

"She was single."

"Boyfriend, then?"

Guzman shrugged. "I didn't know her that well. I didn't ask, either. She worked some of the time in Garcia's. That's the trading post on the south end of the village. You probably saw it when you drove up."

"The place with all the Indian drums and pottery in the window?" Guzman nodded. I patted myself on the back. Now I knew where I'd seen the girl before. Up on the mountain where Cecilia Burgess had been knocked over the guardrail, the light had been poor—just the spotlights and flashlights. And when the girl had been placed on the gurney, her profile had been visible to me only briefly. But it was enough to stir a memory.

Earlier in the day, before I'd started my outdoorsman's hiking act, I'd stopped at Garcia's Trading Post, thinking I might find a birthday present for my oldest daughter, Camile. Odds were good I'd find something that she hadn't seen already in ten department stores near her home in Flint, Michigan.

The polite young lady who'd let me browse without interference through blankets, beads, and jewelry had been Cecilia Burgess. I was sure of it.

"What I mean is that she had the opportunity to see all sorts of people," Guzman continued. "San Estevan is pretty small, but there's still plenty of the young and willing. My nurse said she'd heard Burgess had been seeing a guy from on up the canyon."

Guzman turned and called Mary Vallo, who'd gone back out front. When she appeared in the doorway, Guzman asked, "Who was that kid you said Cecilia Burgess was seeing up north?"

"I don't know his name," Mary Vallo said, keeping her voice and facial expression that wonderful stone neutral that serves Indians as such a perfect barrier when they don't want their minds read.

"Yeah, but wasn't he the one who was living up at the hot springs?"

"I heard that he was," Mary said.

Guzman turned to me. "There's a little group of left-over hippies who camp out about nine months of the year in the National Forest, up behind the hot springs. They drift in and out of town, work a little, panhandle a little, and generally make the tourists nervous. I heard Cecilia Burgess was hanging around with one of them. I never saw him."

"He didn't wash much," Mary Vallo said evenly, and when I glanced up, surprised at her opinionating, all I saw was her back as she retreated back down the hall to the front office.

I chuckled. "Terrific. And hippies? I thought they were twenty years extinct."

Guzman grinned. "Maybe that's the wrong word. But whatever you want to call 'em, then. Squatters. My father used to call them *greñudos hediondos*, but then anyone who drove a van without being a plumber was suspect to him."

"Is there a colony of them up there?"

"No," Guzman said. "Not as far as I know. Just a few

individuals, kids who like to spend the summer sacked out under the stars. Some of them live in tents…some just throw a bedroll under the overhang of a rock." He spread his hands. "It's just some place to stay where they aren't harassed. The only time I've ever heard that the Forest Service forced anyone out of there was when the fire danger got too high."

"Like now?" I asked, remembering the crunch of the needles under my feet.

"This is wet compared to six years ago, according to some of the locals. Ask Mary. I've heard that back then the state cops wouldn't even let you park along the shoulder of the highway."

I fell silent for a moment, deep in thought. "That's quite a hike, from town up there."

"About six miles," Guzman said.

I shrugged. "If you're young, I guess that isn't so bad. Maybe that's what she was doing…hoofing it on up there for a little midnight nookey. Did she hang around with anyone else?"

"No, but as I said, I don't keep a census. You might find some other answers if you check with the Department of Social Services. The girl might have filed for child assistance. And I don't know where the other child is or even *if* it is."

"What other child?"

Guzman frowned and grimaced. "I keep forgetting." He flipped open the manila folder on his desk, and I wondered what else he'd forgotten. After a minute he said, "This isn't the first child she's had." He held up his hands. "I don't know what the story is. Or even if the child, assuming it lived, is here in San Estevan."

"But she did have one."

"Yes, she did."

"Could you tell how long ago? How old the child would be?"

Guzman shook his head. "I'd guess it wasn't more than four years or so."

I started to fiddle for another cigarette and then changed my mind. "So it's possible there's a little kid roaming around somewhere wondering what the hell's happened to his life."

"Possible," Guzman said, and he held up his hands again in surrender. I was about to shoot another question at the tired young physician when I heard the front door open and then the sound of enough boots on the tiles to herald an invasion.

Estelle Reyes-Guzman appeared in the doorway, and behind her were two other uniformed deputies, a state trooper, the same Forest Service employee I'd seen up on the mountain, and one other man in plainclothes. It was that man who pushed his way past all the elbows and gun butts and crossed the office to pump my hand.

"Goddamn, look what crawled in!" Castillo County Sheriff Pat Tate bellowed, and I stood up, hand still locked in his beefy paw. I'd tipped more than a few brews with Pat at law confabs all over the state through the years. "Estelle said you was up this way. How the hell have you been?"

"Not bad," I said.

"No, really," Pat said, squinting at me like I was lying to him. "The heart and all? That's fixed up now?"

"All fixed up. And you?"

"Fine, until I got jerked out of bed. Hell of a note. Let me introduce you, here." He jerked a thumb at first one deputy and then the other. "Paul Garcia and Al Martinez. I think you know Al, don't you?"

I nodded and shook hands. "It's been a while," I said, and Martinez grinned. About six years before, he and I had been involved in a particularly messy prisoner extradition and transfer from my county to Castillo. I was surprised Martinez could still smile when he saw me. As I remember, he'd ended up having to drive the prisoner home in a patrol car that reeked of vomit and it was a six-hour trip. And that was about the best part of the whole deal.

I didn't know the state policeman, a hatchet-faced man of thirty-five or so with eyes like ice chips. The trooper, Bobby Padgett, shook my hand impassively, since Sheriff Tate hadn't told him who I was yet. I didn't figure him for the sort of man who shed any warmth until he had to.

"And you met Les Cook up on the mountain," Tate said, and I shook hands with the pine tree warden. "Gentlemen, this is Bill Gastner, undersheriff of Posadas County, about a thousand miles south of here, down in the frijole district."

Tate looked pleased with himself, stepped back, and put his hands on his hips. He was not a particularly big man, maybe five feet seven and 170 pounds. But he managed to look aggressive with his close-cropped and thinning hair, bulbous nose, and stout jaw. "So, you got this goddamned awful affair solved for us?"

I shook my head and sat down again. Estelle had been using her husband's shoulder as a leaning post, but now she was no longer in the room. I assumed she had slipped out front, either for coffee or maybe to talk with nurse Mary Vallo.

Knowing Estelle, she had thoroughly briefed Sheriff Tate. But she'd still know ten times more than he did. As political as she was, she'd let him lead the way because he was the boss. She'd done the same with me in previous years, making me and the department look good.

"This is a goddamned mess," Tate said and found himself a chair. He looked sideways at Guzman. "Did the transfer to Presbyterian go without a hitch?"

Guzman nodded. "She was losing it, though. Dr. Bailey rode down in the ambulance with her."

"The girl's not gonna make it?"

"No, I don't think so. Short of a miracle."

"That's what Estelle said up on the hill." Tate sat forward on the very edge of the chair, one hand on each knee. He lifted one hand to rub his whiskers. "Estelle said she thinks it was murder." I looked at Francis Guzman and wondered how Estelle had jumped to that conclusion without the medical evidence her husband had gathered.

"That's why she called me up here before the roosters. Hell, otherwise it's just another car-pedestrian accident, and in Indian country they're every other day."

"Had Burgess been drinking?" I asked Guzman.

"Not enough to smell," he said. "I'm sure the medical examiner will order a full workup, though."

"Well then," I said, "the deputy isn't alone in seeing this one as murder. So does the doc here. Tell them what you told me."

Guzman ran through his findings without wasting a word, and Tate listened without interruption.

When Guzman finished, Tate asked to see the X rays. "Huh," he said, standing in front of the lighted viewer.

"That's the sort of damage you'd get in a car wreck, where your knee is slammed up against the dashboard, isn't it? The big leg bone drives backward and smashes the hip joint all to hell."

"Exactly," Guzman said. He shot Tate a look that said he was impressed as hell at the sheriff's acumen. "Or from a very bad fall. Rock climbers, for instance."

"Estelle!" Tate called. He turned to one of the deputies. "She's out front. Get her in here, will you?" He turned back to the X ray. "Knee damage?"

Guzman traced a faint line with his finger. "Fractured patella. Some torsion injury. Lacerations."

"That's consistent, then."

"With a fall," I said. "Not with being hit by a car."

"Right."

Estelle came in, coffee in one hand, cookie in the other. "These are out front if you want some," she said, but Tate's mind wasn't on breakfast yet. "Look at this X ray," he said. "Look at that leg." Estelle did so, then turned to her husband. "Were the neck scratches consistent with fingernails?"

"Yes. I'd say so."

"And I started thinking about the way her clothing was torn," Estelle said.

"What do you mean?" Tate asked.

"A fall down a slope doesn't tear underclothing or the neck of a blouse. Not like that."

"All the girl's clothing went to Albuquerque?" Tate asked Guzman, and the young doctor nodded. To Estelle, Tate said, "You might give the M.E. a buzz and put him on the alert. It might help him find what you need. Make sure he doesn't miss anything." Tate looked out the door.

I could see the other officers clustered around the coffeepot. The trooper was standing in the hall, his back to us.

Tate said, "This mess happened on Forest Service turf, so you keep them informed." He took a deep breath and narrowed his eyes at Estelle. "I'm going to dump this one in your lap, for a couple reasons. Most important, I'm not sure a small, closemouthed community like this one is going to react positively if a whole brigade of lawmen descends on them, tearing the place up and sticking their noses where they maybe don't belong. It's a hell of a lot easier just to shrug and say, 'No se,' than to cooperate with the government. Do you see it that way, Bill?"

"Every time," I said. "And if you get about four agencies trying to work together, forget it."

Tate grunted agreement. "If you need anything, just call. I'm going to assign Paul Garcia to you for a few days. He needs experience, and you can work in plainclothes." He pointed a stubby finger directly between Estelle Reyes-Guzman's dark eyes and added, "And don't you decide to get heroic on me. When it comes time for an arrest, you call me first. Do you hear me?"

"Of course, sir," Estelle said quietly.

"Good." Tate turned around and grinned at me. "How long are you staying up in these parts?"

"I'll probably drive back tomorrow or the next day."

"You mean you're not going to stick around and see the action?"

I grimaced. "Come on, Sheriff. Estelle doesn't need any help from me. And I'm on vacation, remember? The last thing I need is a busman's holiday. There's already been too much excitement around here for me.

All I want is the home-cooked dinner I was promised, and then I'm on my way."

Tate glanced at Estelle as if to say, "You cook, too?" but had the good grace not to. Instead he turned, extended a hand to Guzman, and said, "Doc, can we buy you some breakfast?"

Guzman shook his head. "No, thanks."

Tate then took me by the arm like a comrade of old and ushered me toward the door. "Let's give the man his office back and find us some breakfast burritos. Then I need to get back to the city. Estelle, you need to show Paul your plush office and get him set up."

I should have been flattered that Pat Tate wanted my company, but I knew damn well that breakfast with the sheriff was going to be reminiscing—one war story after another until we'd both drunk enough coffee to ruin a kidney. By then half the morning would be shot.

That was an agonizing thought, because I'd been watching Estelle Reyes-Guzman's face during the past few minutes and wanted more than anything else to hear what was on her mind.

# FIVE

"Do you feel like taking a short walk?" Estelle Reyes-Guzman asked and I groaned.

"Sure. Why not." There were several good reasons why not. Sheriff Pat Tate had finally taken leave around 10:30 that morning, and I was still bloated from the coffee and raw-mouthed from too many cigarettes. When Tate left, I had remained at Bobby's Cafe.

Earlier I had made arrangements to meet Estelle there when she'd finished her errands. The cramped, dimly lighted eatery was across the street from Garcia's Trading Post, and it had been interesting to watch the traffic come and go. In a common enough display of poor sense, when noon rolled around I'd ordered a "Burrito Grande" special for lunch.

I had just finished eating when Estelle's county car swung into the cafe's parking lot and pulled to a stop beside my Blazer.

As she entered the small dining room, I waved her to a seat. That's when she hit me with the invitation for exercise.

"Where are we walking to?" I asked.

Estelle looked at the big plate in front of me and the scattered remains of the lunch. "What was that?"

"It was too much, that's what it was. Burrito Grande I think they call it. And you're as evasive as ever. Where are we walking to?"

"I'd like to hike up to the hot springs camp."

"To talk with Cecilia Burgess's boyfriend?"

"You heard about him?"

I nodded and looked at the bill for lunch. If food that good had been that cheap down in Posadas, I would have weighed 700 pounds. I fished out a tip. "Your hubby knew about him. I asked Francis if the Burgess girl had any other romantic flames besides the hippie. He didn't know."

Estelle nodded vigorously. "She does. Or did. I talked with Mary Vallo…Francis's nurse?"

"I met her." I tucked the tip under the plate and stood up. "Tell me on the way. If I sit here any longer, I'll go sound asleep."

"Mary's born and raised here. She knows every living soul, I think. Anyway, there were some rumors going around that really upset some of the older folks. They'd talk with Mary at the clinic. Apparently Cecilia Burgess was spending some time with Father Nolan Parris. That's what the *solteronas* told Mary."

"Who's Parris?" I paid the bill, and we stepped outside into the bright sunshine.

"He's in retreat. At the Servants of the Paraclete. You might have noticed the enclave just north of the Forest Service office?" I nodded and she added, "Parris and Burgess were seen together on several occasions."

"Whoopee, Holmes," I said dryly. "Maybe they're cousins. Maybe a thousand other possibilities. Maybe Cecilia Burgess went to the good father for confession. Are the little old lady gossips assuming that there's an affair going on? That's pretty thin, Estelle."

"I'm just telling you what Mary Vallo told me. It's another angle." She nodded at my Blazer. "Let's drop that off at my house." I followed her car north until, just beyond the gas station, she turned off on a lane between two irrigated cornfields. A quarter mile farther on, tucked under two massive ancient cottonwoods, was a tiny adobe. Estelle pulled into the driveway and gestured for me to park close to the wire fence. Judging from the outside, the house had four rooms at most. But it was neat and clean, and the nearest noisy railroad or interstate was seventy-five miles away. It would be peaceful as a tomb at night.

"Cute place," I said as I settled into the county car.

"It's cheap," Estelle said. "Until Francis and I decide what we want to do this fall."

"Do?"

Estelle shrugged. "We might not want to spend the winter here. The house has just a couple of those little wall heaters…and they're not much good."

"I don't imagine either one of you is home much."

"No. Especially not this week. But he's always said he wanted to practice in a tiny village."

"He got his wish. This is hardly Denver." We rode silently for a few minutes, and I watched civilization thin as we drew away from the village. "How do you like it here?"

"Interesting," she said. "It's quite an experience being the only cop in town. You wouldn't believe some of the domestic disputes I've been called to."

"I think I would. What do the *solteronas* think?"

Estelle grinned. "About me, you mean?"

"Uh-huh. If the old maids are upset at the idea of a woman talking to a priest, what must they think about a female deputy sheriff?" She didn't answer right away, and I added, "Has there ever been one around here?"

She shook her head. "I don't think so."

"I imagine that takes some adjustment." I stretched to ease the seat belt tension on my full stomach. "They'll get used to it, like anything else. And in time, they'll all wonder how the hell they ever did without."

"I don't know," she said. "My mother isn't used to the idea yet."

I knew Felipina Reyes pretty well. The old woman, a widow for twenty years, lived alone in Tres Santos, a tiny village thirty miles south of the U.S.-Mexican border.

When Estelle had worked for me in Posadas, she was only an hour's drive north from her mother, but to Felipina Reyes, her daughter might as well have worked on the moon.

And ay! To be carrying around a revolver as an *agente del Alguacil Mayor de un contado en los Estados Unidos! Double ay.*

"So what else did you find out this morning?" I asked.

"Well, I talked with Orlando Garcia."

"Who's he?"

"He owns Garcia's Trading Post, right across from where you were eating."

"Son of a gun. I never saw your car over there."

Estelle grinned briefly and left me hanging. Maybe she could go invisible; I don't know. "Garcia had a lot to say about Cecilia's boyfriend up at the springs. Not much of it good."

Before she had time to elaborate on all the juicy particulars, we reached the turnoff. She swung the patrol car into the campground below Steamboat Rock and then drove to the far end of the parking lot. A grove of runty Douglas firs would provide enough shade to keep the Ford from turning into an oven.

The trail east to the hot springs followed a small stream that ran into Isidro Creek. We walked slowly in deference to the discomfort in my gut. After a couple of minutes, I felt better. Maybe there was something to this exercise business. I even had enough breath for a question.

"What's the boyfriend's name? Did Garcia know that? Mary Vallo never said."

Estelle nodded. "H. T. Finn."

"H.T.? I wonder if his mother named him Huck and he couldn't stand it."

"Maybe. Garcia didn't know what the H.T. stood for."

"How old a guy is this Finn?"

"Orlando wasn't sure. Older than thirty, though. And that sort of surprised me."

I took a deep breath. "Hiking this trail will keep him in shape, that's for sure."

We skirted the buttress of Steamboat, a massive volcanic plug that rose vertically from the canyon and towered upward for nearly 300 feet. The trail was well worn and marked further with a considerable collection of refuse. Beer and pop cans, gum wrappers, cigarette packs, diapers…you name it.

After a hundred yards the trail forked and the Forest Service sign announced that the hot springs were three-quarters of a mile to the left, with Quebrada Mesa a mile and a half to the right. Of course I noticed morosely that the trail to the hot springs angled steeply uphill.

We trudged a hundred yards and I stopped to catch my breath. "Are you all right?" Estelle asked.

"I'm fine," I gasped. "Just fat. And I smoke too much."

Estelle grinned. She gestured ahead and said sympathetically, "I think it levels out just up ahead." It did, but not nearly enough.

The first sign of human encampment was a site tucked under a limestone overhang, with the recess sheltered on either end of the overhang by mixed oak and aspen. Smoke from campfires had blackened the overhanging rock, and I guessed that if a scientist could find a way to section that smoke residue, there'd be traces dating back hundreds, maybe thousands of years.

It would have been a favored spot for any hunter passing through, from yesterday's hippie back to Pueblo Indians before him and then back to whoever came before the ice age.

A sleeping bag was rolled up tightly and stuffed well back under the rock. Estelle crouched down and pulled out the bag. A quick examination produced only a well-worn flashlight and a half roll of toilet paper.

"They travel light," I said. Estelle pushed the bag back where it had been. "Are there other sites on up ahead?"

"Yes," she said. "That's where most of them are. Right by the springs."

Another fifteen minutes answered my question. The hot springs formed a series of stair-stepped pools, nestled in a grassy swale. The overflow burbled downhill, forming a tiny rivulet not more than two feet wide. Thickly timbered saddlebacks rose steeply on either side of the swale. Any wind would have to do some serious corkscrewing to reach campers down in that protected place.

A gigantic boulder rested like a granite house near the first pool. And I would have missed him had Estelle not stopped suddenly. I followed her gaze and saw the young man sitting on top of that boulder.

He was sitting Buddha-fashion, legs crossed, and wearing only a pair of cutoff jeans. As we stepped closer, I saw he had a book open in his lap. He watched us approach without any obvious interest or movement. When we were a dozen feet away, we stopped. I had to crane my neck back to look up at him and felt foolish.

"Good afternoon," I said.

"Hello," he replied. He was so scrawny his ribs looked like they might pop through his skin. Long snow-colored hair hung down to his shoulders, and even if he'd given up most of society's conventions, he certainly hadn't lost his comb. His hair was placed just so...like he'd finished giving it the hundred strokes with the comb moments before.

"Beautiful afternoon, isn't it?" Estelle said, but the boy's only reply was a slight toss of his head to move a fall of hair farther from his eyes. "Are you H. T. Finn?"

"No."

"Is he still camping up here?"

The boy's eyes darted off to one side, to glance at the big tent that was pitched up at the head of the swale. He was a miserable sentry, and I figured that he'd lie, too. He did. "Nope."

"Do you know where he went?" The boy shook his head.

At that moment we both heard the voices, first that of a small child, then the faint mumble of an adult's reply. I turned and looked north, past the tent and on up the saddleback. Two figures were walking slowly down through the timber, and by squinting I could make out a man and a small child, hand in hand.

"That's maybe him?" I said, ignoring the boy on the rock.

"Could be," Estelle said quietly. "Or maybe just hikers."

"She's a little small to hike so far from the parking lot," I muttered when I could see the child more clearly.

Estelle turned and looked intently at the boy up on the rock. He'd closed the book at least. "Is that Finn?" she asked, and her voice carried some authority. The boy finally nodded, and Estelle turned back to me. "Well, technically, Finn isn't camping at the moment, just as his friend here said. He's hiking. Let's go have a chat with him."

# SIX

H. T. FINN nodded at me without much interest, but for him Estelle Reyes-Guzman was another story. He eyed her as if he were choosing another member for his harem.

Normal interest was certainly excusable, since she wasn't wearing the starched and quasi-military duds that sheriffs' departments favor...and those, along with a wide Sam Browne belt loaded with hardware, take most of the sex out of the figure.

But Finn's gaze started at Estelle's running shoes and drifted slowly upward, pausing here and there until I was ready to slug him.

Finn was no kid. I guessed him to be within shouting distance of forty. He wore blue jeans torn at each knee and a gray T-shirt. On the T-shirt was one of those fish symbols with the words JESUS CARES stenciled underneath.

He was fit. The T-shirt stretched over a wide chest and powerful shoulders, with no bulge at the waistline. And he was either tough or heavily into pain, because he was barefoot. I winced at the thought of walking over the limestone-studded forest floor without something to protect my soles.

I glanced at the child...a toddler, almost. She was a pretty tyke with golden hair parted down the center and pulled back into a thick ponytail. Big, trusting blue eyes watched Estelle without blinking.

Her red jumper needed a washing, but at least she was wearing shoes. Her hand was tightly clutched in his. She edged closer to his leg and started to back around behind him when she saw me looking at her.

"Mr. Finn?" Estelle asked.

"Who are you?" Finn grinned, still letting his eyes drift.

"I'm Deputy Estelle Reyes-Guzman, Castillo County Sheriff's Department. This is Undersheriff Bill Gastner."

I didn't bother to correct Estelle's implication that I was on home turf. Finn wasn't impressed anyway. "You have some identification, I assume?" he asked, still grinning. At least he had enough control over his hormones to raise his eyes from Estelle's chest to her face. The grin was only from the nose down—his gray eyes were void.

"Yes." Estelle pulled out her wallet and held it up so he could see her badge and commission. He glanced at it briefly, then looked at me. He raised an eyebrow.

"Pretend that I'm a civilian," I said. If I had to arrest this son of a bitch, that would be soon enough to show him anything. His eyes narrowed.

"Mr. Finn, we'd like to talk with you for a few minutes," Estelle said.

"So talk," Finn replied. "This is National Forest land. They let anyone in." He flashed that humorless grin again.

"I understand that you knew Cecilia Burgess?"

Finn hesitated only a second before nodding. "Yes. I knew her."

"She came up here from time to time?"

"Of course." He said that as if he thought us both simple.

"When was the last time you saw her?"

Finn pursed his lips. "Alive, you mean?" His bald-faced response startled me. "Before last night?"

"You knew that she was involved in a pedestrian accident last night?" Estelle asked.

"Yes."

I glanced down at the little girl. She had transferred her grip to the seam of Finn's jeans. And she had given up on us as something interesting to watch. The thumb of her other hand was jammed in her mouth as she watched a stinkbug make its way through the pine needles. All the adult talk was lost on her.

When I looked back up, Finn had clasped his hands together, resting them lightly on his chest like a priest.

"She's still alive, Mr. Finn. At least she was this morning, when she was transferred to Albuquerque." Finn accepted that with a slight nod and spread his hands apart slightly as if to say, "So you say."

"How did you hear about the accident?" I asked.

Finn lifted only one hand this time and pointed downhill at the youth on the rock. He did it slowly and gracefully, again reminding me of a priest, maybe extending the consecrated bread during Eucharist. "Robert was in the village this morning."

"How did he hear about it?"

"You'd have to ask him," Finn said. "But in a village so small news travels rapidly, doesn't it?"

Estelle nodded as if she hadn't thought of that on her own. "How long had you known Burgess, Mr. Finn?"

Finn took a deep breath and gazed off into the distance. "Several months," he said finally. "What's today?"

"August 5."

"Well then, let's see. I first met her just before Christmas. So I guess that's seven or eight months."

"Do you know who else she associated with? On a regular basis?"

Finn looked irritated for the first time. "I have no idea. What she did down in the village was her business."

"And when she was up here?" I asked.

"What do you mean?"

"You and she were close?"

Finn glanced down at the little girl. The tyke had squatted and was nudging the stink beetle with a tiny index finger. The beetle thrust its hind end up in empty threat. "Of course," Finn said after some hesitation. "Otherwise she wouldn't have come up here."

I decided to try a long shot, based on my conversation with Francis Guzman. "Is this her other child?"

"I beg your pardon?"

I knew damn well that Finn had heard me just fine, but I repeated anyway. "Is this child her daughter?"

"No," Finn said immediately. "Ruth is my niece. She spends the summer with me." He smiled faintly. "The city is no place for a child."

I had no argument with that logic. Estelle Reyes-Guzman turned slightly so she could see Robert of the Rock. "Did your friend say anything to you about hearing how the accident happened?"

The smug expression returned to Finn's face. "You'd have to ask him."

This time Estelle came as close to snapping as she ever did. "No, Mr. Finn. I asked what he said to you, sir."

"Nothing, Deputy," Finn said, one eyebrow raised. "If you want to find out what he knows, talk to him."

"We'll do that on the way down. And by the way, do you have some kind of identification with you?"

"Identification?"

"That's right."

"Certainly." He pulled a wallet from his right hip pocket, rummaged for a moment, and then held out a New Mexico driver's license. Estelle took it, pulled out a small notebook from her hip pocket, and jotted down information. Finn waited patiently until she had finished and handed the document back. "If there's nothing else?"

"Thank you for your time," Estelle said pleasantly. Finn reached down and took the little girl's hand, turning to go back toward the tent.

Before the child could turn, Estelle knelt down so she was looking at her squarely in the eye. "What's your name, honey?" Estelle asked quietly.

The tyke hesitated, then responded to Estelle's warm smile. "Daisy," she said with a faint lisp.

"That's a pretty name," Estelle said. She tousled the child's hair and stood up. She smiled at Finn. He frowned, then nodded curtly and led the child back uphill toward the big tent.

"Sweetheart, isn't she?" I said as we strolled down toward the rock. "Finn says her name is Ruth, and she says it's Daisy. And you know something you're not telling me."

"She is a sweetheart," Estelle said. "And I'll bet you twenty bucks that she's Burgess's child. Orlando Garcia knew Cecilia had a child…he'd seen her many times. The child used to play in the back room of the store when Cecilia worked there."

"And her name was Daisy," I said. Estelle nodded, and I continued, "So Daisy is her nickname. And maybe Finn's lying, and maybe he's not. How is it your husband never had occasion to meet the child? Here we are wondering about Burgess's other kid and she's right under our noses."

"She was never sick maybe? I don't know."

"You just found out about her today? When you talked with Garcia?"

"Yes."

"Then I feel a little better."

"We still have a problem though," Estelle said, then dropped the subject as we approached the rock. Robert had started to move when we were fifty yards away. He pulled on a T-shirt, gathered up the book, and dropped off the backside of the rock as agile as a cat.

"Robert," Estelle said as he appeared on the uphill side of the boulder, "did you either witness yourself, or talk to anyone who did, the accident last night down on the state highway?"

"No."

"You just heard about it in town this morning?"

Robert hesitated for just a fraction of a second. "Yes."

Estelle nodded and glanced at me. "Thanks," she said, and Robert almost said another word but thought better of it. "I think we're finished here," she told me, more for Robert's benefit than mine.

When we were out of earshot, she added, "Blabby kid, isn't he?"

"Yes."

Estelle grinned at my imitation. "I'd be willing to bet another twenty bucks he knows lots more than he lets on."

"He'd have to. And did you happen to notice what else was interesting?"

Estelle frowned, and I felt an unprofessional twinge of pride that I had seen something she hadn't. "What do you mean?"

I stopped and looked back up the trail. "He was wearing a gun."

"Oh, that. Yes, I saw the bulge under his T-shirt when he came around the rock." She twisted around and put a hand on the small of her back, where the gun had been.

"When you asked him if he'd seen the accident, he turned a little to face you. That's when I saw it," I said.

Estelle shrugged. "Probably half the people in New Mexico carry guns." She looked back up the trail. "That's kind of interesting, though. A gun in one hand, a Bible in the other."

"Is that what the book was?"

"Uh-huh."

"Couldn't read the title," I said lamely. I concentrated on where I put my feet. It was easier going downhill, but I was top-heavy and needed to watch my step.

"If the child is Cecilia's daughter, it's going to be a mess trying to work through the social services department to get that kid out of the woods," Estelle said.

"Paul Garcia is working on finding Burgess's relatives, if there are any. He should have turned something up by the time we get back."

"And if there aren't any?"

"Then we'll have to work a court order of some sort." I nodded. "You're running on a lot of assumptions."

Estelle held a branch so it wouldn't whip me in the face. "You think she should be living up here? Without her mother?"

"She didn't seem to mind."

"No, maybe not. I do though." She stopped and stood for a minute with her hands on her hips, staring off into space. "Do you think that either Finn or Robert knows who tossed Cecilia Burgess?"

"No, I don't. They would have said something if they did."

"That's what I was thinking."

"And by the way," I said, "I hate to tell you your job, but you didn't I.D. Robert of the Rock. It might have been handy to know who the hell he is."

"I know who he is," Estelle replied and started off on the trail once more. I had to puff a little to catch up.

# SEVEN

THE SUN ROLLED down the edge of Chuparrosa Mesa
west of San Estevan, and the wash of evening light
blushed the sandstone layers below the rimrock into a
dozen hues. The ceramic chimes beside the Guzmans'
front door hung motionless.

I exhaled and watched the plume of smoke curl
through the chimes, to fan out and then disappear into
the *savinos*, the peeled and smooth juniper poles that
lay diagonally across the vigas to form the small porch
roof. I closed the file folder and tipped my chair back
until I could lean against the adobe wall.

"Robert Arajanian," I said and tapped my index finger on the cover of the folder. "And you say that the
guy who owns the trading post—Orlando Garcia—he
knows him?"

Estelle Reyes-Guzman returned from the kitchen
and handed me a mug of coffee. "Yes, he knew him
by name. He'd had the opportunity to cash a couple of
checks for the kid."

"What kind of checks?"

"The only one he remembered for sure was one
made out to Cecilia Burgess. It was her tax refund
check. For just a few dollars, as far as Garcia remembers. Burgess had signed it over to Arajanian. Orlando
Garcia didn't seem to approve much. I got the impres-

sion that he thought Cecilia Burgess was wasting her time with both Arajanian and Finn."

I opened the folder once more. "That seems to be a generally held view around here. Odd that she signed the check to the kid instead of her boyfriend Finn. Maybe the trio shares everything." I read the file. "And Arajanian has quite a record."

The folder had been delivered from Albuquerque earlier that afternoon by a deputy. It had been on Estelle's desk when we returned from the hot springs, and it made interesting reading.

Robert Arajanian had experimented with the law when he was just fourteen…an assault charge filed by the parents of another high school student. I noticed the other youngster involved had been seventeen— either he'd been small for his age or a complete wimp. Or young Robert had been spectacularly aggressive. Less than a year later a charge of vehicular homicide had landed Robert Arajanian in a youth detention home for two years.

"Interesting that he wasn't drunk for the vehicular charge…or at least there's no mention here that he was," I said. "The implication is that he used the damn car as a weapon."

"He was drag racing and bumped the competition into a grove of pine trees."

"Where's it say that?"

"It doesn't. I called Albuquerque while you were in the shower."

"You don't waste a second, do you?" I looked at the file again.

"So he gets just two years for what is essentially murder."

Estelle moved her Kennedy rocker so that she could

put her feet up on a big planter that supported one sorry-looking beavertail cactus. She shrugged at my comment. Under New Mexico law two years was the most detention any kid got, no matter what the crime, as long as he wasn't tried as an adult. I grunted with disgust. Murder could come pretty cheap.

After his release from the detention home, Robert Arajanian had remained clear of the law for four years. Two days before his nineteenth birthday, and eight months previous to his playing lookout on the hot springs rock, the kid had been charged with misdemeanor possession of marijuana and attempted burglary of an apartment in the Northeast Heights of Albuquerque. He'd pulled six months probation for the marijuana. The attempted burglary charge never went to court.

"Well, that's neat," I said. "He must be a slick talker, too, when the spirit moves him. The burglary complaint was withdrawn. His first chance at a good, solid felony as an adult and someone wimps out. So now he can possess a firearm legally. Otherwise, as a felon, he'd be in violation."

"There probably wasn't enough evidence to make the burglary charge stick. Who knows?"

"So," I said. "All very interesting, but nothing yet on H. T. Finn."

"Albuquerque didn't have anything on him. It's going to take a while to track him down, I suspect." Estelle sounded disappointed—as always, hating unanswered questions.

"What do you think the odds are that either Arajanian or Finn or both pitched Cecilia Burgess over the embankment?"

Estelle grimaced impatiently. "Zero."

"Really? Finn didn't seem awash in grief at the news of the accident. In fact, he seemed to assume that she was already dead." She shrugged. "And he didn't say anything about going into the city to visit her either, but what does that prove?"

"That he doesn't like talking to strangers, especially the law, or that he doesn't have a car."

"He could hitchhike. The Indians do it all the time. Do you need more coffee?"

"No, thanks." I sat silently as she got up and went inside. I heard the coffeepot clank against the stove burner, and she started talking before she was out of the kitchen.

"I don't know why we're even worrying about Finn and Arajanian anyway. What we need—" She was interrupted by the telephone. I heard her monosyllabic side of the conversation but what I heard was enough. When she hung up and returned to the porch, her face was sober.

"She died?"

Estelle nodded. "At six-sixteen p.m." She glanced at her watch. "Twenty-two minutes ago."

"What's your next step then?"

She sat down in the rocker and gazed off toward Chuparrosa Mesa. "Someone must have seen her shortly before she was struck. Did someone pick her up in the village? Was she walking up to the hot springs?"

"Late at night?"

"Who knows. And we don't know what time she was hit either. She could have been lying there for some time. It had to have taken her some time to crawl up to the highway."

"It's hard to imagine, the way she was hurt."

"Sheriff Tate said that they're still in the process of running a complete background on her. He'll let me know." She made a face of frustration and leaned forward in the chair. "Not a single piece of evidence to tie in a vehicle of any kind, Tate said. No paint chips, no nothing. And…"

"And what?"

"And that's not what really bothers me."

"What does, then?"

"Daisy bothers me, sir."

I said nothing and watched Estelle's face as her agile brain sifted the facts.

She shook her head after a minute. "I hate to think of her up there with those two creeps."

"We don't know anything about Finn, Estelle. He says he's the girl's uncle. If he really is, the Department of Social Services will never give you a court order unless you can prove abuse or neglect or something like that. And if Finn's lying to us, it'll still take a while for a court order. And there's one other possibility, too."

"What's that?"

"We don't know for certain that the child is Cecilia Burgess's daughter. We're making an assumption just because her name is Daisy."

"Come on, sir," Estelle said in a rare display of contention. "Who else would she be? Coincidence is one thing, but that would be ridiculous. She even looks like Cecilia."

I held up my hands in surrender. "I couldn't tell you. And little kids all look alike to me. I'm just tossing it out as another possibility, that's all. Farfetched, but a possibility. And maybe Finn is telling the truth. But trust Tate to dig it out. He's a ferret." I sighed deeply and stretched. "I'm glad it's not my worry."

Estelle looked at me over the top of her coffee cup. "Give me another dozen hours, and you'll be so tied up in this case you won't be able to sleep at night, let alone go home." She grinned. "*Como dos y dos son quatro*, as *mi madre* would say. And besides, I need your help."

"Yeah," I laughed. "Another hike like today's and you'll be attending my funeral. You've got Deputy Garcia. Walk his young legs off."

"Exactly," Estelle said. "We're going to find an eyewitness if we have to talk with every soul in this valley. Everybody. I asked Paul to talk with as many folks as he could, to see if anyone remembers catching a glimpse of a vehicle late last night. Especially a pickup."

"There's thousands of pickups around here."

"We have to start somewhere."

I nodded and listened to a long, plaintive growl from my stomach. "And when do we eat?"

"As soon as Francis comes home."

I groaned. "My God! We have to wait on a country doctor? It's apt to be midnight. I'll be dead by then."

Estelle laughed. "I'll get you a beer, some chips, and salsa. That'll tide you over. Really, he won't be long."

She got up and said over her shoulder as she disappeared into the house, "And I need to ask you a favor."

"What's that?"

"Just a second." After a bit she returned and set the promised snacks on the porch floor beside my chair. She handed me the beer. "I need you to talk with somebody for me."

"Who?"

"Father Nolan Parris. At the retreat house."

I regarded Estelle with interest. "He's the monk or friar or whatever you call 'em who was hanging out with Cecilia?"

"According to rumor."

"He might know something. I wonder if he drives a truck."

"A priest? No, I don't think so."

"Well," I sighed, "it's a place to start."

Estelle grinned. "It'll give you something to do."

I shrugged, convinced for about thirty seconds that the reason Estelle Reyes-Guzman was asking me to talk with Parris was because of the vast years of experience I had under my belt. And then, looking across the porch in the failing light and seeing the last bits of summer sunshine play around the planes of her face, I realized Estelle's request was astute. If she arrived at the Catholic retreat complex in uniform, there'd be talk. If she strolled in to visit in civvies, there'd be even more talk, all of the wrong kind. What could be more innocent than one old man visiting another?

"It'll cost you several beers," I said. I expected jocular agreement, but Estelle shook her head.

"We need to talk with Parris tonight." She pulled a small photograph from her blouse pocket. It was a picture of Cecilia Burgess, the posed kind with the misty background that college yearbooks favor. "Make sure he looks at this." She handed the picture to me. "See if you can get him to hold it just the way you are right now."

I frowned. "Where'd you get this?"

"She lived in one of the small back rooms at the trading post when she wasn't up at the springs with

Finn. Garcia let me in. There wasn't much there. Just some clothes and things. The picture was being used as a page marker in a children's book."

"And you want Parris's prints?"

"I want a thumbprint."

"Parris doesn't have any kind of record where his prints were taken? Passport, anything like that?"

Estelle shook her head. "Not that we can find."

"And what good will his prints do, anyway?"

"Remember the guardrail? The bloody prints, top and bottom? We assumed Cecilia Burgess somehow pulled herself over or under the rail."

"You're telling me the prints we saw aren't hers… she had help?"

"That's right. The prints aren't hers. That's what Sheriff Tate told me over the phone when he called to tell me Burgess died."

"What about that guy who stopped and called on the CB radio? Maybe he tried to help her."

"He said he didn't. And he's a state employee. Works in the Department of Revenue and Taxation. His prints were easy to double-check. He's clean."

"And no luck on what's his name, with the Forest Service? He was there before you were."

"Les Cook? He's a cop. Not a chance."

"Then someone else was there and split," I said. Estelle nodded. "Might have been the driver of the vehicle, maybe someone else." I cleaned off the photo with my handkerchief and carefully slid it in my pocket. "I'll get Parris's prints for you. And I suppose this means we're going to have to walk all the way back up to the hot springs, too."

"The prints don't match Arajanian's. Tate already

checked for me. We don't know about Finn. So yes, we need to go back." I groaned at the thought of this exercise business becoming a habit.

# EIGHT

ESTELLE AND I ate dinner without her hubby. Francis called from the clinic just about the time Estelle had to turn on some lights so we wouldn't trip over the furniture. He'd been about to leave for home when an Indian woman walked through the door with a sick youngster.

The stoic little kid had been flinching from a middle ear infection for several days, and the infection had bloomed. When his temperature spiked through 104 degrees, the mother decided herbs weren't enough. The kid had himself a fine case of infectious meningitis.

Estelle sighed with resignation when Francis told her he wouldn't be home much before midnight. After the youngster was transferred to Albuquerque, Francis wanted to follow up with a visit to the pueblo to see with whom the kid had come in contact.

The two chatted for a few minutes, and when Estelle hung up I smiled. "Marry a doctor and you starve to death."

"Usually, it's me who gets called out at all hours," Estelle replied. I leaned against the refrigerator and watched her cook. The kitchen was as tiny and cramped as the rest of the house, and I took it in at a glance. The row of bottles on the narrow windowsill above the sink surprised me—a whole alphabet of vitamins, minerals, and human fuel treatments. I reached over and picked up the largest, a collection of vitamin E capsules.

"I thought you always said that green chili cured all," I said. She glanced my way and I put the bottle back.

"Francis wants to make sure the baby gets everything he needs," she replied as offhandedly as if she'd remarked on the weather.

She laughed at the blank look on my face and went back to chopping onions.

"Well, congratulations," I said. "When?"

"When what?"

"When's it due?"

She took a deep breath. "February 10."

I laughed. She even had that event pegged to the day. "That's great. Does Sheriff Tate know?"

Estelle shook her head. "Francis and I agreed that I'd go on leave in October. That's soon enough."

"Then what?"

"We're not sure. I don't think I want to work." She grinned widely. "I don't think I want to face the wrath of *mi madre*. She'd never speak to me again if I left her grandson in a day-care center."

"You two will work it out I'm sure," I said. I picked up a loaded plate and carried it over to the table. She'd called it frijoles con something, and the food was so damn hot I accused her of serving it with a sauce of lit gasoline. But the spices—and the news about the pending kid—perked me up.

As we ate, our conversation kept circling back around to Cecilia Burgess and her boyfriends. Estelle wanted me to visit Father Nolan Parris, and there was no better time than that evening.

Shortly before nine, feeling fat from too much high-octane dinner, I arrived at the retreat complex just north of the village. As the crow flies the place was less than a mile from Estelle's home.

The center included several small buildings clustered around a large three-story house. Monstrous cottonwoods shaded the complex and blocked out what little light there might have been from passing traffic, the moon, or even starshine.

Estelle hadn't needed to worry about being seen by the wrong folks if she visited Parris. It was too dark for starting rumors. I parked the Blazer behind an older model Fairlane station wagon. A single bulb beside the double front door of the main house illuminated enough of the siding and porch to show that the facility was well maintained. I opened the door of the Blazer and listened. The compound was stone quiet. Maybe the clergy were in the middle of their late evening services.

The three raps of the brass knocker were loud enough to make me flinch. I formed a mental picture of a row of bowed, maybe even shaved, heads snapping up at the sound and nervous hands clutching rosaries.

The retreat was for clergy who had strayed from the straight and narrow. Some may have nipped the bottle too often...maybe a few dallied with members of the fair sex—or even with their own sex. "I think it's sort of a second chance house," Estelle had said and that made sense. If a priest couldn't concentrate on his prayers here, he was probably out of luck.

The right-hand side of the double doors opened and an elderly cleric peered out at me. I shouldn't say elderly...hell, he was about my age, maybe a year or two younger. He wore basic black, without the Roman collar.

"Good evening," I said and held my identification

up so he could see it through the screen door. I adopted my most accommodating tone. "I wonder if it would be convenient for me to visit with Father Parris?" The priest squinted at the badge and commission card, and I wondered if he could read it well enough to see the county name.

His watery gray eyes flicked from the identification to my face, and I put the wallet away. "Well," he said and placed one hand on the screen door like he was preparing to push it open for me, "this isn't the best of times."

"I won't need much of his time," I said. "And it would really be a help."

He started to push open the door, then asked, "You may have to wait a moment or two. May I tell him who's calling?"

The doorkeeper had just flunked the reading test. I could just as easily have held up my Sears card. "Undersheriff Bill Gastner." He'd forgive a minor sin of omission. I opened the screen the rest of the way and stepped inside.

"If you'd care to wait here, in the front room?" the priest said, indicating a small parlor crowded with overstuffed furniture and a small upright piano. "I'll fetch Father Parris." He touched my elbow lightly as he guided me into the room and then left.

I thrust my hands in my pockets and gazed around. I stepped over and perused the titles in the single bookcase. Most were Reader's Digest chopped editions. If the good fathers had a theological library, this wasn't it. I turned at the sound of footsteps. "Father Parris will be down in a few minutes," the priest said and smiled. "Can I get you a cup of tea or coffee or something?"

"No thanks. Appreciate it though."

He nodded and left. I sat down in one of the chairs and found that it supported me in all the wrong places. I perched forward on the edge of the cushion, clasped my hands together, rested my forearms on my knees, and waited. After about two minutes, I noticed that there were no ashtrays in the room. I took a deep breath and occupied my mind by trying to imagine what Parris looked like. In another minute, I had my answer. My guess hadn't been close.

Nolan Parris stepped into the doorway of the parlor and stopped. He rested a hand on the jamb. He was short, no more than five feet five and handsome in a well-oiled sort of way. His black hair was carefully trimmed with the part just off-center, and he kept the sideburns short. He wore gold wire-rimmed glasses, and his brown eyes glanced around the room when he first came in as if I might have company hiding behind the furniture.

I guessed that he was no more than thirty-five, just beginning to soften around the edges and expand at the gut. And he was pale, like a man just risen from bed after two weeks with the flu.

"Good evening," he said cautiously.

I rose and extended my hand. "Father Parris?"

"Nolan Parris, yes." He entered the room and limped to the center of the carpet, where I met him. His perfunctory handshake expended two pumps. "Do I know you?"

Once again I pulled out my identification. Parris looked at it and a muscle in his jaw twitched. He nodded and gestured toward a chair. "Please."

"Father Parris, I'm assisting Deputy Guzman with

an investigation of a pedestrian accident earlier today up the canyon." A pained look swept briefly across his face. He was wearing slippers, and his right sock was bulging around what was probably an elastic bandage. I didn't know if the grimace was because of the ankle or my announcement. "Perhaps you heard about it."

He nodded. Something was interesting in the pile of the old purple carpeting in that room, because that's all Parris was looking at. "I heard about it, yes."

"Would you take a look at this, please?" I held out the picture of Cecilia Burgess, and Parris took it. With satisfaction I saw his thumb clamp down on the bottom margin of the photo. "Do you know the young lady?"

"Yes, of course, Cecilia Burgess. I've known her and her family for years." He took a deep breath, held it, and slowly let it out with a slight shake of his head. He handed the photograph back.

"Her family? She has relatives in the area?"

Parris shook his head. "No longer. Her parents died when she was quite young. For a time she was living with her brother in Albuquerque."

"Where's her brother now?"

"Richard's dead. About five years ago."

"How did that happen?"

Parris took his time collecting his thoughts before he said, "He was riding his motorcycle on Central Avenue in Albuquerque. A pickup truck ran the red light at Washington. Richard wasn't wearing a helmet. It probably wouldn't have done any good even if he had been."

I grimaced. "Hard luck family. And he was her only brother? No others? Sisters?" Parris shook his head. "What did the brother do?" Parris glanced up at me, puzzled. "His line of work?" I added patiently.

"He was a priest." Parris hesitated and watched me pull a small notebook out of my hip pocket. When my ballpoint was ready, he added, "We attended seminary together."

"He was older than Cecilia?"

"Yes. By about twelve years."

"What was your relationship with Cecilia?"

Parris eyed the carpet again. "We were good friends. As I said, we'd known each other for years."

I paused and stuck the pen in my mouth. "Father Parris, are you aware of what happened last night?" Parris nodded. His eyes were closed. I waited until he opened them and looked at me. "Would you tell me how you found out?"

Parris slumped back in the chair, and his left hand strayed to his pectoral cross. He toyed with it for a minute, then clasped his hands together. "I heard all the sirens, of course. And then this morning I had occasion to drive into the village. I sprained my ankle last night, and I needed an elastic support. Orlando Garcia, at the trading post, saw me and asked if I'd heard."

"And what did you do then?"

"I called the clinic immediately."

"Do you remember what time that was?"

Parris pursed his lips and glanced at his wristwatch, as if the hands might have stopped at the moment in question. "Midmorning. It was shortly after I'd finished mass here."

"And then?"

"They told me that Cecilia had been transferred to Albuquerque. To Presbyterian. I drove into the city immediately."

"So you were aware of the extent of her injuries?"

Nolan Parris stood up with a grunt and limped across to the bookcase. He rested both hands on the top shelf for support. I waited. Finally he said, "I administered last rites. I was there when she died." He turned and looked at me without releasing his grip on the bookcase. "I made arrangements. A friend of mine at Sacred Heart will say rosary and mass, probably tomorrow. I did all I could. And then I drove back here."

"Father, are you aware that Cecilia was pregnant?"

"Yes." His lack of hesitation surprised me.

"Do you know who the father was?"

"I'm not sure I understand how that is relevant to the investigation of the accident," Parris said without much conviction.

"Do you know?"

He pushed away from the bookcase and sat down on the only straight-backed chair in the room. "I can't imagine what good these explorations into Cecilia's private life can do now."

"Father Parris, a hit-and-run is homicide." Parris's face flushed, and his shoulders sagged a little. "So you see, information of any kind might be helpful to us."

Parris bowed his head, and for a moment I was afraid he'd sunken into one of those hour-long prayers. Eventually, he looked up at me. "Yes, I know who the father was. Or I should say, I know who she said he was."

"And who's that?"

"A fellow by the name of Finn."

"First name?"

"I'm not sure. They're just initials I think. H.P. maybe. Something like that."

"Are you aware of where Mr. Finn lives?"

"Oh, he lives around here, all right." Parris almost chuckled, the sound coming out like more of a snort. "Up at the hot springs. He and a *friend* camp out there." He stressed the word *friend*.

"Do you know the friend?"

"No. But I've seen him once or twice. And Cecilia mentioned him now and again. A younger man, I believe."

"And so you think Finn is the father?"

"Cecilia said he was. She said he paid one or two of her bills at the health clinic."

"Did Cecilia Burgess have any other children?"

The question seemed to catch Parris off-guard. He watched the rug patterns for a long minute, then settled for a simple shake of the head. A very small shake.

"So the little girl who's staying with Finn—Daisy, I think her name is—isn't Cecilia Burgess's child?"

"No, not as far..." Parris stopped abruptly. His face was anguished. "No, I'm not going to do that." He was speaking more to himself than to me, and I remained silent. His features twisted with some internal struggle, and I thought for a moment that the young priest was going to weep.

He closed his eyes again for a while, then got out of the chair, limped to the door, and gently closed it.

"I'm sorry," he said quietly. "Forgive me. This is hard." He made his way slowly to the chair nearest mine. I said nothing, letting him take his time. He surprised me with a faint grin. "I feel as if I'm in the confessional."

"Some different laws apply," I said gently.

He nodded sad agreement with that. "The girl living with Finn is my daughter."

"And Cecilia's?" I prompted.

"Yes," Father Nolan Parris said. He looked relieved.

# NINE

OVER THE YEARS, I've had lots of practice at not looking as surprised as I felt. This was one of those times. I leaned back in the chair and regarded Parris with interest. Then, trying to sound fatherly instead of intimidating, I said, "So tell me."

He shrugged. "It's no long story. As I said, Cecilia's brother was a close friend of mine. My best friend. We'd known each other since we were two. We went to school together, all the way from kindergarten through college and seminary." He stopped, arranging his mental cards.

"I wish some of his willpower and discipline had rubbed off on me. I drink too much, Sheriff. Or at least, I did." He clasped his hands tightly together. "I guess that I was an alcoholic by the time Richard Burgess was killed. That's what they tell me. Anyway, his death…the stupidity of it…the waste…was all the excuse I needed.

"I don't remember all the grim details, and I don't think I ever want to. The next eighteen months were my own private hell. They say a drunk has to hit rock bottom before he'll admit to being in trouble." He shook his head. "Do you know where they found me, finally?"

I shook my head and Parris said, "I was living in a cardboard box under an Albuquerque overpass—

downtown, where the old railroad station used to be. And *living* is probably the wrong word. A rookie cop happened by and he thought I was dead. Next best thing. They took me to St. Joseph's, and one of the nurses recognized me…she remembered when Richard Burgess and I hung out together. We used to be on rotation together as police department chaplains. *Los dos padres*, they called us. But that was a long time ago." He hesitated, lost in his memories. My back hurt from sitting so long.

"I didn't have any close relatives. Just one cousin back east somewhere. The nurse knew about Cecilia Burgess and called her. That was the big mistake, I guess. That's when it started. I held onto her like a damn leech. I guess I put her through more hell than even last night."

"I doubt that."

"Anyway, one thing led to another. I was an accomplished liar. Always have been. I could lie to myself as easily as to anyone else. I made up some of the most wonderfully creative stories…personal sob stories that suckered that poor girl right into my world. I guess it was one of those nights when she was trying to keep me from tearing the apartment apart…that's when we started."

"You had sex with her, you mean?"

"Stripped of all the niceties and excuses, that's the gist of it."

"And that guilt really set you off?"

Nolan Parris looked up sharply at my tone. He moved his jaw sideways, assessing me. "Maybe you don't understand, Sheriff. You impress me as the kind of man who's always known exactly where he stood, who always knows exactly what he believes."

"I've had my moments. Anyone does. But that's not what's at issue now. I gather the two of you didn't stay together long?"

"No. I can remember having long discussions with her about my leaving the clergy, after finding out she was pregnant. But I…I just couldn't."

"Why not?"

Again Parris looked at me critically, but he wasn't in a hurry to answer. To let him off the hook a little I asked, "How did the two of you end up here, in San Estevan?"

"She took some courses at the university, and one of them involved a field trip to the mountains around here…geology, I think it was. She fell in love with the village and had dreams of raising Daisy here, away from the city."

"Daisy's the girl's name?"

"Yes."

"When did Cecilia move up here?"

"About a year ago."

"And you?"

"Me? I received the ultimatum from my bishop last August. Dry out or get out." Parris smiled faintly. "Bishop Sanchez didn't use those exact words." He shrugged. "I've been here ever since. I could have left long before, but I'm serving as a resident counselor."

"And you've stayed dry?"

Parris nodded slightly. There wasn't any pride in his voice when he said, "Dry."

"Good for you. Even today?"

He covered his face with two smooth hands and then

cupped them under his chin. "Even today. Falling off the wagon wouldn't have done Cecilia any tribute."

How noble, I thought. "What's Daisy doing up at the hot springs with Finn?"

I couldn't imagine leaving a kid of mine on the mountain with a long-haired freak while her mother expired in a hospital a hundred miles away...even if I were a priest and inordinately sensitive about appearances.

Parris's face hardened, and I noticed the tick in his cheek again. "You have to understand, Sheriff, that even though we live in the same village, Cecilia and I see little of each other. We saw little of each other. For very obvious reasons." He stopped in case I had to ask what the reasons were. I didn't. "And she had been living with Finn, off and on. And was to have his child." He held up his hands helplessly. "Now you have to believe I was going to—"

We were interrupted by the sound of a powerful car's engine as the vehicle slowed and then lunged down into the retreat's driveway. The flash of headlights stabbed through the window and then I saw the wink of blue and red.

"What the hell..." I said, rising to my feet. I peered out through the window and saw Estelle Reyes-Guzman's county car as it nearly climbed the steps. "Excuse me." I yanked the parlor door open, then the front door, and met Estelle just as she reached the porch.

She immediately turned around and headed back for the car, saying over her shoulder, "Come on, we need to get up the canyon." I turned to Parris, who'd limped to the door and was standing behind me. "Don't go away," I said and then made for the car. Estelle had already yanked the Ford into gear, and as soon as my ass dropped into the seat, she slipped her foot from brake to accelerator. The cruiser kicked gravel all the way out to the highway. "What's up?" I said as she got the car straightened out and howling on the pavement.

"Paul Garcia thinks he's found the pickup truck." Estelle Reyes-Guzman's voice was charged with excitement. She was riding the cop's high that comes when a burst of new information cracks a case wide open and makes the adrenaline flow. I stayed quiet, not wanting to distract her. I didn't want the county car plunging into the canyon. Besides, I was feeling a little let down. Here I had spent an evening pumping gossip out of a priest, and a rookie deputy sheriff had gone and solved a murder case.

# TEN

I DIDN'T NEED to see the speedometer to know that the county cruiser was rocketing up Isidro Creek canyon fast enough to turn us both into jelly if we ran off the pavement.

If we didn't wipe out a tourist family just as they pulled out of a campground, it would be a deer standing stupidly in the middle of the road just after a corner, blinded by the lights and spellbound by the noise.

Estelle held the steering wheel tightly in one hand, and with the other she played the powerful spotlight along the sides of the highway far ahead of us. Her jaw was set in determination. I reached back and groped for the seat belt, then pulled it around my girth and snapped it tight.

We entered a long straight stretch and I asked, "How does Garcia know it's the truck?"

"He spent the afternoon dogging after someone who might have seen something...anything. I guess he hit paydirt. Pat Waquie said he'd seen a blue over white Ford half-ton cruising around the village last night."

"Who the hell is Pat Waquie?"

Estelle didn't answer for a moment as she paid attention to a series of S-curves. Then, as calmly as if she were selling stamps, Estelle said, "Pat lives in that rambling adobe just beyond where the pueblo land starts.

He has the orchard where the trees practically hang out over the highway." She glanced at me to see if I was following her description.

I gestured at the highway. The white lines, what few there were between long strips of double yellow, blended together into one racing stripe.

"So how does it figure to be the truck we're after?" I asked.

"Garcia's hunch. Waquie remembered it because one of the guys in it tossed a beer can in the old man's front yard. Waquie was sitting on his front step enjoying the evening when the Ford drove by. They were really whooping it up."

"Living by the highway, he must get lots of that."

"This time, it was his own nephew."

"And how…" I stopped as the Ford blasted toward a sign that announced a tight switchback. The yellow sign called for fifteen miles an hour. I tried to push both feet through the floorboards, and one hand reached for the dashboard.

Estelle hung the big car out wide, braked hard, slapped the gear selector down to first, and when the rear end howled and broke loose punched the gas. We exited the corner as pretty as you please, straight in our own lane and accelerating hard.

"…how does that connect with Burgess?"

"Garcia said the old man told him that he'd seen the nephew drive by a couple of times, each time a little faster and noisier…and the kid had picked up some passengers. The last time, well after dark and just before the old man went inside, he saw his nephew go by with at least five in the truck...three inside and two in the back."

"The old man notices the fine details," I said, skeptical.

"That's what he said he remembered. And the boy's been in a couple good scrapes before. His folks let him run wild. The uncle doesn't like it much, but what can he do?"

"So based on the old man's tale, Garcia thinks that maybe Cecilia Burgess got herself picked up by a bunch of drunks and ended up raped and in the rocks."

"It's possible."

"It's as good as anything else you've got." We hit a straight stretch for a few hundred yards, and I tried to relax. "Where's Waquie's nephew now?"

"He's with the truck."

"And Garcia's sitting on him somewhere up here? He's got him staked out?"

"Right. So to speak." We had reached the head of the canyon, and the stop sign at the T-intersection shot past as we swerved out onto the main state highway that ran east-west through the mountains. The convenience store off to the left faded behind us as we headed east.

Estelle said, "A group of Girl Scouts found the truck. They're camping out on the backside of Quebrada Mesa. As the crow flies, it's only a mile or less to the scout camp over on Forest Road 87."

"What do you mean, 'found the truck'? Crashed, you mean?"

Estelle nodded. "And let me guess. The kid's inside it."

"Apparently." Estelle suddenly stood on the brakes, and we skidded to a stop in the middle of the highway.

"I missed the turn," she said, and we backed up so fast my forehead almost hit the dashboard.

"Christ," I gasped. "If your kid ever wants to be a damn racing driver, you'll know where he got the notion." My neck snapped back as she braked our backward plunge.

Off to the right, a small Forest Service sign announced: QUEBRADA MESA CAMPGROUND, 7 MI., and SNAKE RUN TRAIL, 4 MI. Below that, it said: PRIMITIVE ROAD—NOT MAINTAINED. We jolted onto the forest two-track, and if I'd worn dentures, they would have been in my lap.

"We're not going to the campground," Estelle said as if that made everything hunky-dory. "The scouts are a couple of miles this side of it, where the mesa edge is right next to the old logging clearing."

She was already assuming that I knew the country as well as she did. I let it ride and concentrated on keeping my head from being driven through the roof of the Ford. In a couple places, the road would have been narrow for a three-wheeler, and the low-hanging ponderosa pine branches wiped scratches the full length of the patrol car. A limb as thick as my thumb whacked the mirror on my side askew and screeched across my window.

"Guzman, this is Garcia." The radio message cracked loud despite the bouncing car, and I reached for the mike. I wasn't about to give Estelle an excuse to take her hands off the steering wheel.

"Go ahead, Garcia."

We hit another rut and I almost dropped the mike. Garcia's voice was loud and clear. "I can hear you coming up the two-track. Estelle, stop where the scouts are.

There's a washout or two farther on. You'll break an axle if you're not careful."

"Ten-four. Appreciate the thought," I said, and to Estelle, I added, "I wonder if he broke his."

For another five minutes we crashed along the path. Then Estelle swung the Ford around a corner and slewed the car to a stop. Four Girl Scouts stood in the middle of the lane, terrified. The lights from the roof rack pulsed across their faces.

The oldest kid couldn't have been fourteen, and I wondered where their counselor was. "We can park right here," Estelle said. She switched off the car and the lights. "…if you don't mind hoofing it for a few yards."

"No, no. I don't mind," I said and popped my seat belt before she changed her mind.

"The other officer told us to meet you out here," the oldest scout said as Estelle got out of the car.

"Good girls," Estelle said. She snapped on her flashlight. I was still rummaging, and Estelle called, "In the glove compartment." I found the other flashlight and grunted my way out of the car. It felt good to plant both feet on unmoving ground.

"Where's the other deputy?" Estelle asked, and the scout pointed off to the west.

"It's shortest this way," the girl said. "Part of the road farther on is washed out pretty bad. We can cut straight across." There were six of us and six flashlights, and still the timber was dark as tar. I brought up the rear, hoping that the five young ones in front of me would kick all the obstructions out of the trail. They left enough to keep me paying attention.

This particular portion of Quebrada Mesa was a

narrow spit of land where the two sides of the mesa tucked in tight before fanning out to blend with the swell of the mountain behind it. The Forest Service two-track was an access road to an old timber sale area. Campers used it and maybe serious lovers who didn't want to be disturbed. I couldn't imagine casual drinkers jolting their innards just to quaff a brew under the moon.

We reached the edge and as we paused for a minute, I could hear the faint shush of wind through the pines below us. "Where's Garcia?" I asked.

"Down this way," the brave scout said, and we walked along the edge single file. A hundred yards ahead I saw several lights gathered at the edge and then, when the timber thinned some more, I saw a single flashlight down below, fifty, maybe sixty yards away. It had to be a hell of a drop-off.

Four more scouts and two counselors waited for us. The counselors—two gals of maybe eighteen or twenty—looked as scared as the little ones. Estelle looked down and then asked, "Is there an easy way down there?"

"It's all pretty steep," one of the counselors said. "The other deputy just slid down from here."

Estelle sighed, and I knew what was going through her mind. She didn't like someone skidding willy-nilly through the middle of her evidence. She pulled the hand-held radio from her belt and keyed the button.

"Paul? You copy?"

"Ten-four."

"We're up on the edge above you."

"I see the lights." His flashlight swept an arc for us. "What have you got down there?"

"One nineteen-seventy-six Ford half-ton, blue over white. As far as I can tell, there were just the two occupants."

"All right. I called Dr. Bailey from Jemez. He's covering for Dr. Guzman tonight. He's our closest. It'll be a half hour at best."

"Ten-four."

Estelle turned to me. "I called for ambulance and coroner before I picked you up. But it's going to be a while. Do you want to go down or stay here?"

"Should you be doing stuff like this?" I asked and knew right away my concern was a waste of breath.

"Come on, Padrino," Estelle said. She grinned. "The kid may want to be a mountain climber someday."

I grunted disapproval, at the same time swelling a little with pride that when Estelle had finally called me something other than "sir" it had been the Mexican equivalent of "godfather."

"Let's do it," I said. Skinnying down into that black void wasn't my idea of a good time, but what the hell. When her child was born, I didn't want him looking up at me from his cradle and saying *wimp* as his first word.

Estelle swept the ground with the flashlight. "Paul," she said into the hand-held radio, "did you locate exactly where the truck went over?"

"About fifty feet south of you. To your left."

"Ten-four. We're going to look around up here a little; then we'll be down."

"We ain't going anywhere."

Estelle included all the scouts in her flashlight arc. "Maybe you girls would go on back out to where I parked the car. An ambulance and other personnel will be following us in, and we don't want them going any further than we did." That would be a real trick, since the fat rump of her patrol car was blocking the two-track. The girls started to move off, and Estelle added, "And we'll want to talk with you all, so don't go anywhere else."

I heard a "Yes, ma'am," from one of them, and then we could see their flashlights bobbing as they made their way back through the big pines.

"Hell of a way to spend a campout," I said. "Imagine the ghost stories you could tell 'em now."

"And you'd have wet sleeping bags for sure," Estelle muttered. "Let's see where it went over."

I took a deep breath, suddenly and deeply feeling fatigue as it snuck up and clubbed me. Being an insomniac is one thing, but I'd been on my feet, one way or another, since the accident sirens had awakened me at the campground. And this was the second time I'd been stumbling around in the dark, peering at evidence with the feeble light of flashlights.

"I wish to hell you'd learn to work during the daylight hours," I said as Estelle made her way along the rim to the south, her light sweeping the ground.

"No time like the present," she said cheerfully. "And here we go." The tracks she had found were faint impressions in the soft duff. Estelle followed them with the light. The tracks came from off to the left, from the old two-track.

Her flashlight beam reflected off the white of Garcia's four-wheel-drive Suburban. The road he had driven wound down through the trees from where we had parked, then looped over toward the mesa rim forming a turnaround that the logging trucks had used years before.

The driver of the pickup had driven straight across the turnaround and held course for the vertical drop-off...and as tired as I was, even I could see that not once had he spiked the brakes before going over.

# ELEVEN

THE PICKUP TRUCK lay on its side at what we later measured as sixty-three yards below the mesa rim. I pictured the Ford crunching almost lazily off the precipice. The undercarriage had scraped the rocks as the truck tipped over, so it certainly hadn't vaulted off like something driven by a Hollywood stuntman.

Fifteen feet into the plunge, the truck had hit a small juniper and twisted sideways, beginning the first of several rolls. On the second roll, the windshield had smashed against a large limestone boulder.

The trail of glass followed the truck's course downward from when first the back and then the side windows had shattered. Forty-one yards from the rim, the truck had flopped on its back on an outcropping that almost stopped the trip.

But inertia won, and the Ford had tipped on over, dropping eighteen feet straight down. It landed on its left side, rolled twice more, and finally wedged to a stop against a collection of housesized boulders.

It wasn't so clear what had happened to the occupants. The first was lying where he'd been crushed when the truck smashed into the outcropping.

The kid…he wasn't much more than that…had been sieved through the space between the collapsing cab roof and the dashboard on the driver's side. The blood, tissue, and clothing fragments on the rocks told a familiar story. The truck had held onto him for one full roll and then tumbled on, leaving the crushed and torn rag doll behind.

"What I.D. did you find?" Estelle asked Paul Garcia.

"I haven't touched anything yet. I didn't look."

Estelle nodded, and I held the light for her while she pulled out the kid's wallet. She handled it carefully, just with the very tips of her fingers. "Robert Waquie," she said and looked up at me. I snapped open her briefcase and handed her a plastic evidence bag, and she dropped the license and wallet inside.

"So the old man called it right," I said.

"Yes, it appears so. Paul, where's the other one?"

Garcia twisted and pointed downhill, off to the south. "Over there about twenty yards, almost on a line with the truck."

"You're kidding," Estelle said and stood up. "There's no way he could have been thrown that far, and certainly not in that direction." I was the only one who took time to find an easy way around the outcropping…Estelle and Garcia went straight down the rocks like goddamn mountain goats.

The second victim was as dead as his companion. From what we could tell, his injuries were consistent with being bashed around inside a crushed cab.

"He was extruded out through the back window," I said. I held my light close and pointed at the crescent-shaped piece of Plexiglas that was driven into the small of the victim's back three inches above the belt. I swept my light back to the truck, pointing it at where the custom sliding camper window had been installed in place of the solid glass window. Most of the window's aluminum frame had been torn from the cab.

His I.D. said Kelly Grider, and he had lived long enough to pull himself a few yards away from the wreckage, and then he'd bled to death.

Estelle stood near the corpse. Several times she flicked the light from Grider to the truck, as if trying to outline the path crawled by the victim. "What do you think?"

"You sure pick 'em," I said. "They had to have been drunk to pull a stunt like this."

"They were drunk all right," Estelle said. "I can smell it on both of them."

"And the truck's loaded," Paul Garcia offered. "Empty cans, a couple of empty bottles. A couple of six-packs waiting to be opened. They had to be so stoned that they just idled right over the edge."

"Easy enough to do if you're not paying attention," I said. "But why were they up there in the first place?"

"Scout hunting, probably," Estelle said.

"Then the scouts are goddamned lucky," I muttered. To Garcia, I said, "Did you take a good swing around the area? No other surprises?"

Garcia shook his head. "No, sir. I spent an hour down here, and I spent it looking. Not a thing. Just the two."

"How did the scouts come across this in the first place?" Estelle asked.

"They're on a campout just down the mesa. They said about a mile or so."

"Then they probably heard this."

"They said no. Apparently, they were taking a night hike up the canyon bottom."

"A night hike?"

"Scouts do that," Estelle said. "So they were down this slope even farther than we are now."

"That's what the counselor said. They were following the watercourse, and one of them flashed her light up here on the slope. That's when they saw the truck."

"Damn strange place to hike," I said.

"Not really, sir," Estelle said. "The watercourse follows the bottom of the ravine and gradually slopes up until it joins the mesa almost at the two-track where we came in. So you can hike it and know right where you are when you surface. Good for orienteering."

"And they didn't think the wreck was just a leftover from the logging days?"

"It was steaming," Paul Garcia said.

"Steaming?"

"Yes, sir. That's what they said."

"What did they do then?"

"A couple of them climbed up to the wreck, saw what it was, and then the whole squad beat a trail back to the main camp...straight east as the crow flies. There's a good trail the scouts have made. They use this mesa all summer. So it's not bad hiking, even at night."

"Especially when you're in a panic," Estelle observed. "And they called you from the camp."

"That's right. They gave me directions to find the two-track turnoff from the main road, and they met me right where I'm parked now."

"I'd think half the camp would be out here," I said.

"The head counselor of this group said the camp director and assistant director are in town for something. She thought it best to keep it kind of quiet until we had a chance to see what's what. She didn't want to upset the kids any more than she had to. So she kept her group together and kept a lid on things."

"Make sure she gets a medal," I told Estelle. "Her kind's rare."

"That's for sure." Estelle pinned the truck with her flashlight beam again, then swept the light up the steep slope. "Let's get some pictures and measurements before the coroner gets here."

I left the legwork to the youngsters…Garcia didn't even breathe hard as he worked the idiot end of the tape measure up and down the rock- and stump-strewn path down which the truck had plunged.

I concentrated on the truck. And I thought about Cecilia Burgess. If she had ridden in this vehicle earlier, who had pitched her over the side…Grider? Waquie? Old Man Waquie had said there'd been five kids in the truck when it disturbed his peace…where the hell were the others? Had they ridden up here on this remote mesa, too? Or had they ditched from the joyride sometime earlier?

For many minutes I just sat on a rock, my light beam playing around the inside of the bent, twisted truck bed. Plenty of blood smeared the remains of the rear window and the top rails of the bed…but that could be— and probably was—Kelly Grider's. With better light we could establish blood tracks. We'd see exactly where he crawled and be able to estimate just about how long it took before he collapsed and died.

Far in the distance a coyote yipped. It was a lonely place to die, and I felt a touch of sorrow for Waquie and Grider. But as drunk as they had been, maybe there'd been no chance for reflection.

I grunted to my feet. Estelle was starting her photography, and I let Garcia work the lights for her.

"I'm going to work my way back up to the car," I said. "Our traffic is due and they might want to talk with us on the radio. The hand-helds don't reach out so good."

"The scouts could use a little company, too," Estelle said, then added, "Are you all right?"

"I'm fine. Just tired. I need to sit on something soft and think for a while."

Sixty yards is not all that far, but I had to stop half a dozen times for breath. By the time I reached the mesa rim, my heart was pounding in my ears. I was so tired I almost turned the wrong way, but caught myself with a start.

I didn't try the short cross-country route through the trees but stuck instead to the two-track. I skirted Garcia's Suburban, saw that there was enough starlight, and flicked off the flash. I sauntered along the Forest Service road until I reached Estelle's patrol car.

The scouts were seated in a group under a huge ponderosa, and they stopped their quiet discussion when they saw my dark figure loom out of the darkness.

"Who's the head counselor?" I said, keeping my light off.

"I am," she said quietly and held her flashlight up so that the beam just nicked her face.

"You did good," I said. "We appreciate all your help."

"It's awful, isn't it?"

"Yes, it is. But you did all you could."

"When will we be free to go back to our camp?"

"You're still going to spend the night out here?"

The girl—I couldn't tell much about her in the faint light—almost chuckled. "Nobody's going to get much sleep tonight, so we might as well not get any out here as back at base."

"Well, the young woman detective is going to want to talk with all of you, but as long as we know where you are, I don't see any problem."

"You just follow this road another mile beyond the turnaround," she said. "That's where we'll be, then."

I opened the door of the patrol car, rolled the window down, and sat down. As the scouts filed out, I said to the counselor who brought up the rear, "You kids stay together tonight. Don't anyone go wandering off."

"No fear of that," she said quickly.

The scouts stuck so close together they looked like a single shadow, moving on twenty legs down the two-track. Exhausted, I leaned back against the seat. I must have dozed off, because I startled when the red lights of the ambulance bounced off the rearview mirror and winked across my face.

# TWELVE

Dr. Elliot Bailey was a man after my own heart. He stood on the edge of the mesa and looked down into the black void where flashlight beams zapped this way and that, punctuated periodically by the fireball of Estelle's electronic strobe.

"If you think I'm going to jump down there, you're nuts," he said. Both he and Francis Guzman had arrived on the heels of the ambulance, and on the short hike to the mesa edge from where they'd parked Bailey complained to me about every stick and root underfoot. Maybe he figured none of the young pups would listen.

Guzman and Bailey were opposites. The older doctor was a little gnome of a man, not much more than five feet tall. He wore one of those canvas fishermen's hats, and when he swept it off to rub his forehead, I saw that he was bald as an egg.

"What do you think, Francis? Go ahead and bring the bodies up?" He patted his belly, not eager to risk that investment on the sharp rocks below. That's what ambulance attendants were paid for.

I interrupted before Francis could answer. "I think Estelle wanted one of you to answer some questions down there before they're moved. Francis, I'll show you the way if you want."

"You sure you want to go back down there?"

"Hell, it's easy going down," I said with more confidence than I felt.

"If I break my neck, I'm going to sue the county for every penny it's got," Bailey said, but he followed us. The ambulance crew, four of them, lugged the body boards and other paraphernalia.

They discussed using ropes but agreed finally that the darkness made the slope look worse than it was.

We skirted the rocks that formed the vertical drop-off.

"I don't believe this," Francis said. He spotted Estelle and shook his head. "You sure pick the spots, Officer."

"I was afraid you'd still be busy at the pueblo."

"Oh, I wouldn't have missed this for the world." He pointed his flashlight downhill and sucked in a breath. "Wow."

"How's the little boy?"

"Meningitis is the pits, that's for sure. But he'll be all right. What have we got here?" Francis knelt beside Robert Waquie's corpse. "Did you I.D. this one?"

"Robert Waquie. From the pueblo."

"I know his family," Guzman said as he examined Waquie's face. He pointed to a recent scar over Waquie's left eyebrow. "He did that earlier this summer when he put his dad's truck into a wash south of San Estevan." He twisted and played his flashlight back up the rocks, then down the hill at the tangled pickup. "From what I can see, Estelle, his position is pretty consistent with this kind of incident."

"He's not the one that concerns me," Estelle said quietly.

"Oh." Francis let that pass and continued his examination. Bailey bent over and assisted, the two of them reeling off all the gruesome medical details of what the Ford had done to Waquie. "So he would have died instantly," Estelle said when they paused.

"Absolutely," Bailey said. "He might as well have been lying in front of a steamroller. Same results."

Francis Guzman motioned to the attendants, and while we started down to the truck, they prepared Waquie's corpse for the rugged trip up to the ambulance.

Estelle let her husband and Bailey examine Kelly Grider's remains without interruption for a few minutes, but I could see by the intent expression on her face that she was eager for them to reach the same conclusion she obviously had…whatever that was. They left the piece of Plexiglas in place for the M.E. Bailey lifted the corpse carefully at the hips when they rolled Grider over so the glass spear wouldn't be damaged or moved.

Francis Guzman held the light close and examined the corpse's upper extremities, working his way to the head. He checked the pupils, then moved the corpse's skull carefully. "Huh," Francis said finally. "Go ahead and put him down," he told Bailey. He squatted back on his haunches and looked at the other doctor. "What do you think?"

"I think he was bleeding to death when he crawled out of the truck," Bailey said. "He was about exsanguinated by the time he got here. What surprises me is that he made it this far."

Estelle stepped closer. "I don't understand why he crawled over here, though."

"What do you mean?"

"I'd think someone hurt that badly might try to

make it out of the vehicle, but why crawl off in a random direction? The only way there's help is up the hill."

Bailey frowned at her. "Come on. When a person's hurt that bad, they don't think. They're crawling away from the pain, is all. Just motion. You ever see a dog get his legs busted by a car and then drag himself sideways? Where's he going? Nowhere. Just away from the pain. And this kid didn't crawl through the window. He was thrown out...or most of the way out, anyway."

"His neck's broken though," Francis Guzman said. He touched the base of Grider's skull with his index finger. "Feel right there." Bailey frowned and placed his hands gently on either side of Grider's neck as Guzman moved the skull.

"Son of a bitch," Bailey said. "You're right." He looked up at Estelle. "Third or fourth cervical. The autopsy will tell us for sure. But if the fracture is as complete as it feels, then he didn't crawl an inch after it happened."

"Now wait a minute," I said. "You're saying an injury like that is instantly fatal?"

"No, I'm saying that it's probably instantly and completely paralytic," Bailey said.

"Then if it happened in the wreck, we should have found him immediately beside the truck."

"Or half in and half out," Estelle observed. "But the blood trail clearly shows he crawled over here. You can see the bloodstains on his clothing...the bleeding is spread all the way to his shoes, and to me that's consistent with crawling and hemorrhaging."

"You can't crawl with a broken neck." Bailey shrugged.

"If you want a best guess, I'd say someone caught

up with him…just about here. And finished him off."
Francis Guzman hesitated before continuing. "There's
no other visible neck trauma associated with this fracture. It's done neatly, like someone knelt on the victim's
shoulders, took his head in hand, and pop." He stood
up. "And that takes a lot of strength."

"Is there any other way it could have happened?"
Estelle asked.

Francis shook his head. "If there is, it's beyond my
imagination. It's too bad this didn't happen in the middle of a nice mud flat. Then you'd have some footprints
to help out." He looked first at Estelle and then at me.
"But there was a third person around here. Bet on it."

"You might want to be real thorough when you dust
that truck for prints," I said to Estelle. "If that Ford
didn't go over by accident, then something has to show
up. It's too heavy to push, but maybe on the gear knob
or door handle. Something."

Estelle took a deep breath. "It wasn't an accident."
She examined her flashlight as if the answer were
printed on the aluminum tube. "I want the autopsy report on these two the minute it's finished." She looked
up at me. "And the doors are locked."

"Locked?"

She motioned with her hands. "The lock buttons on
the pickup are punched down."

"I know what locked means, Estelle," I snapped.
"What I meant was so what?"

"Can you picture a couple drunks, out on a lark in
the middle of the forest, being so safety conscious that
they lock their doors? If they did that, they would have
worn their seat belts, too…and that's absurd. And doors
don't lock themselves."

"You're saying that someone didn't want these two popping open a door when they started over…assuming they were sober enough to think of that. But those locks could have been punched down when those kids were flailing around inside, on the way down."

"Maybe. Maybe. But I don't think so. A warm summer night, no wind…why were the windows rolled up, too? Why would they do that?"

She had a point. "It wasn't because of mosquitoes." I looked up the hill and my fingers fumbled for a cigarette. I snapped my lighter and then a thought brewed in my mind that must have been a holdover from my Marine Corps days. I snapped the lighter shut, wondering if the son of a bitch was out there in the dark somewhere, standing behind a tree, watching us.

# THIRTEEN

"THEY HEARD A COUGH?" Sheriff Pat Tate frowned at Paul Garcia. The Girl Scouts had been chauffeured off the mesa and their camp director told to keep all the youngsters on camp property until our investigation was finished.

Deputy Garcia consulted the notes he'd made during an hour spent with the youngsters. "Yes, sir. That's what the counselor said. They were on a night hike, right up the watercourse. They'd been singing to chase away the bears, she said."

"Jesus," Tate muttered. He stood by the tailgate of the pickup truck, trying to make sense of the surrealistic scene. Off to one side a gasoline generator he'd heisted from the highway department chugged away, and the big flood-lamps washed the mesa side in white light.

"Girl Scouts do things like that," Estelle said. "So what's with the cough?"

Garcia continued, "They heard the noise, and one or two of them turned their lights up the hill. That's when they saw the truck. One of them said she could see a wisp of steam coming from it."

"So they went up to investigate?"

"Yes, sir. The counselor said they could hear the engine pinging, like it was cooling. And then they saw Waquie's body. They took one look and lit out to camp."

"I bet they did," Tate said. "So it could have been Grider, still alive."

"I don't think so," Estelle said. "The scouts climbed right up here after they saw the truck. I don't think Grider would have coughed after his neck was broken...I think they heard the killer."

Tate thrust his hands in his pockets and said to Francis, "I told downtown that I want the preliminary autopsy report on Grider sent up by courier just as soon as they have something. But you think it was murder?"

"Yes."

Tate nodded absently. "No other possibility?"

Francis had been in the middle of a yawn, but he stifled it and shook his head. "None that I can think of." We were all too tired to be creative. Old Doc Bailey had been the only smart one, going back to town with the ambulance and the two corpses.

"Stranger things have happened," Tate said. He looked across at me as I lit a cigarette. "Gimme one of those." I handed him one, and he took his time. "Hell, textbooks are full of incidents when a soldier suffered some hellacious wound that was bound to kill him, but he kept right on...maybe hundreds of yards."

"Anything except a broken neck," Francis said. "If the spinal cord is torn, no amount of desire or wishful thinking is going to make it possible to crawl anywhere."

"So assuming all that's true, how did the killer get up here, and how did he get away without being seen by the scouts?"

"We don't know," Estelle said.

"And what the hell's the motive? Hell, these two were nothing but a couple wild-hare kids. Who'd kill them?"

"We don't know that either."

Tate crushed out the cigarette in exasperation. "But you think this is the same truck involved in the girl's death last night?"

"Yes, sir."

He turned and regarded the truck. "Then the connection is there somewhere. Somewhere. Make sure you don't miss one square inch on that thing. We want prints, and we want good ones. If there was a third person up here, maybe he touched something. Maybe we'll get lucky."

The deputies didn't miss. Five of us swarmed over that truck and used enough print dust to powder a thousand faces. I worked as long as I could, but after a while my eyes refused to focus.

I sat on a rock off to the side and watched. Francis Guzman had stayed with us, and as the clock ticked toward three in the morning he finally lost his patience. I saw him escort Estelle away from the truck, and for several minutes the two were in animated conversation. I didn't want to eavesdrop, but I found myself watching like some damn Peeping Tom.

Estelle stared at the ground as Francis talked, and at one point she looked up at him and shook her head. That set off another long session of lecture, and finally she nodded. Francis didn't look pleased. Their faces were only inches apart, and after a minute Francis put one hand under her chin, lifted her head, and kissed her lightly.

The young physician started up the hill, and Estelle walked slowly over to join me.

"Francis is going back to town if you want a ride," she said.

"No. I may go up and grab the backseat of your car for a few minutes after a bit. But how about yourself? You're pushing pretty hard."

That earned me a raised eyebrow, and I guessed that Francis had said much the same thing. Estelle changed the subject.

"Tell me what Parris said." She sat down beside my rock.

"Cecilia Burgess's little girl is his daughter."

Estelle's mouth opened slightly, her lips forming a silent whistle.

"He said that?"

"Yes." I told her about Parris's friendship with Richard Burgess and the priest's sorry affair with the girl after Richard's death.

She looked back over at the truck, lost in thought. "Maybe he'll try for custody now." She turned back to me. "He's got to understand that Daisy is ultimately his responsibility. He can't just give her away. He can't just leave her out in the woods with Finn. Not with her mother dead."

"The kid's the least of your worries right now," I said. "She's happy chasing toads and beetles." I gestured at the truck. "You need a motive. And my first question is simple. If this is the truck involved in Cecilia Burgess's death, what's the connection to this mess? Neither Parris nor Finn had the time or motivation to act out of revenge…assuming that somehow either of them knew who drove the truck."

"You don't think so?"

"No, I don't. Finn didn't appear to give a shit, one way or another. I don't know what his trip is, but he didn't seem too concerned when we talked to him. His focus seemed to be the little girl."

"That's what worries me," Estelle muttered.

"Trust the child's judgment, Estelle. You saw the way she clung to him." She wasn't convinced, but I continued, "And Parris is a marshmallow. It takes a special kind of monster to break a hurt kid's neck in cold blood. Nolan Parris certainly isn't the one." I realized how silly that sounded as soon as I said it. The history of crime was full of innocuous-looking little schmoes who turned butcher.

"We need time to process the prints," Estelle said. "There's got to be an answer here." She stood up. "And I still think you're wrong about Daisy, sir. She doesn't belong in a tent out in the middle of the woods with a couple of Jesus freaks who probably aren't even related to her."

The vehemence of her remark took me by surprise.

# FOURTEEN

We abandoned that damn mesa at seven in the morning. I'd had so much coffee I couldn't go ten minutes between visits to the bushes. My eyes were open all right, but behind them my brain was comatose.

It felt good when the tires of Estelle Reyes-Guzman's patrol car finally turned onto the pavement and we drove back to San Estevan.

She had a briefcase full of fingerprint cards and not much else. We sure as hell weren't dealing with one of those nut cases who hangs signs all over his murder saying, "Catch me, catch me."

Sheriff Pat Tate wanted us all to meet for breakfast and a strategy session, but as we rolled through the village I could see Estelle had other plans. We passed the lane that led down to their adobe. Without slowing the car, she glanced at me and asked, "Do you want me to drop you off at the house?"

I should have said yes just to see if she'd really turn around. Instead I said, "That depends on what you're going to do."

"Francis has a low-power stereo microscope at the clinic that I want to use. For a preliminary print comparison."

"Are you going to eat?"

"I'm not hungry. Maybe after a little bit."

I sighed with resignation but had enough sense to

keep my mouth shut. "I'll tag along. If I go with Tate, I'll eat another of those breakfast burritos, and it'll sure as hell kill me."

We drove through the village, and I noticed the parking lot of the San Estevan Catholic church was full. "Wedding, do you suppose?"

Estelle laughed quietly. "You *are* tired, sir. This is Sunday morning."

"Oh." I looked at the date window of my watch. "Son of a gun. Is the clinic going to be open?"

"I have a key. And Francis might be there."

Francis wasn't there. If he had any sense at all, he was home in bed. To keep myself awake, I made a pot of coffee while Estelle set up in the examining room.

The viewer was designed for counting bacteria colonies growing in petri dishes but worked just fine for ogling fingerprints. She pulled out the card with Cecilia Burgess's prints and then selected through the prints lifted from the truck.

For a long minute she focused and arranged until she had the two sets side by side. Then she just sat and looked. I waited patiently and found it was more comfortable to wait with eyes closed. "Take a look," she said. Her voice startled me, and I realized I'd been asleep. She got up to give me room.

I'm glad the scope had two eyepieces…that way, it supported my head when I leaned over to look. If I had had to close one eye, the other would have followed suit.

In the forty-one years I had been in law enforcement—twenty in the marines and twenty-one for Posadas County—I had looked at thousands of impressions left by human fingers, some of them in unlikely places.

When I looked at fingerprints long enough and often enough I found that it was very much like looking at human faces.

They're all unique, yes, but there are family portraits where similarities show up. All that's required is a clear print—smudge it, and the personality vanishes.

The prints on the left had been provided by the Office of the Medical Examiner. They'd been lifted from Cecilia Burgess's corpse. All ten digits were clear, the prints marred on three fingers by trauma associated with the crime.

I shifted the cards and looked at the prints Estelle had taken from the top right bed rail of the truck. My pulse picked up a few beats. "Huh," I said and shifted the cards. Estelle remained silent and then I heard her leave the room. I could smell the coffee, but what I was looking at was even more interesting.

"The coffee's at your left elbow," she said when she returned.

"Thanks. This is remarkable, you know that?"

"They're clear. It's a good thing the top edge of the truck's bed was clean."

"It usually is. That's where everybody leans when they're standing beside the vehicle yakking. It rubs off the dirt. Now if I had to read a story into these, I'd say that I can imagine a match. We've got a right index, ring, and middle finger and a smudged fragment of the little finger."

"With no trauma."

"That's right. I can't swear to any of the others, but the comparison of the two index fingers would stand up in court. The laceration cut deeply, but just above the center most characteristic swirl."

"That's what I thought."

I looked up from the scope. "She grabbed the side of the truck...and the print position shows she had to be facing forward at the time. Sometime after that, she was assaulted and pitched out. The fingers were cut in the process."

Estelle pushed the coffee cup toward me and indicated a brown bag. "Some of Mary Vallo's cookies left over from yesterday." Cookies weren't my idea of breakfast.

"So she was in that truck for sure," Estelle added. "That's one square of the puzzle that fits." I moved and let her rearrange the evidence under the stereo scope.

"I'm most interested in the prints along the truck bed," she said as she worked. "That's what's going to tell us who was in the back with her."

"Or who killed Waquie and Grider," I added. I looked inside the paper bag. The cookies were those big oatmeal creations that kids hate...and that mothers make so that the cookie supply will last more than a single day. I took one and tried to pretend that it was a bowl of hot oatmeal with brown sugar.

For fifteen minutes I watched Estelle work, trying this card and that. I was just crushing out a cigarette when she sat back, frowning.

"What's the matter?"

She groaned. "Maybe I'm wrong." She leaned forward and concentrated on the scope, but now she had my full attention.

"Wrong how?"

"You look."

I played musical chairs again and found myself comparing the top half of a perfect print on the left with a full but slightly smudged version on the right. The smudges weren't so bad that I couldn't extrapolate how the lines continued. "I'd bet they're the same. I could be wrong, but I'd bet they are."

I straightened up and rubbed my eyes. "'Course, two of almost anything would look the same to me right now."

"I think it's a match."

"Fine. Who do they belong to?"

"The half print is from the graduation photograph of Cecilia Burgess. It's the one that they brought up from the lab early this morning."

My brain was slow to digest that. "You handed the picture to Nolan Parris," Estelle continued, "and that's his thumbprint. Only the top half...like anyone does when they want to pick up a piece of paper carefully by the edge."

"And the other one?"

"From the truck. The right side. Two feet behind Cecilia's."

"Son of a bitch."

"It was oriented the way it would be if Parris had taken hold of the truck side when he was standing beside it. Four fingers inside, thumb outside and pointed to the left and slightly downward." She walked to the sink and grabbed the side, her thumb on the outside. "Like this."

"Son of a bitch," I said again. We looked at each other for a long minute. "That leaves a big question."

"Yes, sir. It does."

"When did the good Father Nolan Parris grab the side of that truck? Here in town? On the state highway? Or up on Quebrada Mesa."

Estelle nodded. "Let's go ask him."

"On a Sunday morning a priest shouldn't be hard to find." I stood up slowly and said more to myself than to Estelle, "And maybe I can find out how he actually sprained his ankle."

"I beg your pardon, sir?"

I waved a hand wearily. "I'll tell you on the way."

# FIFTEEN

When we started to pull out of the clinic's parking lot, Estelle radioed the county dispatcher to let the office know she was bound for the Catholic retreat north of the village. The radio cracked the burst of static that was characteristic of the signal hitting a repeater tower somewhere, and almost immediately the dispatcher was back on the air.

"Four-o-two, ten-nineteen San Estevan."

"Tate's waiting for you at the office," I said. "He's going to want to be briefed on what you've got."

"I was going to stop," Estelle said. "Either there or the restaurant, whichever."

I laughed. "Sure you were."

"I was." She glanced at me, mock hurt. Only a state police cruiser was parked in front of Bobby's Cafe, so Tate wasn't lingering over breakfast. The party was at the highway department building. I counted six vehicles that belonged either to Castillo County or the Forest Service.

Inside Estelle's closet-sized office, the air was thick with smoke. She propped the door open. I lit a cigarette in self-defense.

Pat Tate was looking at a wall map with two of the deputies, tree warden Les Cook, and another serious-looking young man in pine-tree green. Deputy Paul

Garcia was sitting at the single desk, frowning over paper work.

"We wondered where you went," Tate said when he turned around and saw us. "You missed breakfast."

"No, I didn't. I had a wonderful cookie while she matched prints. The clinic has a good viewer."

"What did you find out?" he asked Estelle.

She put her briefcase on the desk where Garcia worked. "First of all, it is the truck that was involved with Cecila Burgess's death. We lifted a perfect print of hers from the truck bed."

"She might have touched it some other time," Tate said.

Estelle grimaced. "No. I think she was picked up, probably here in town. Maybe she was hitching up to the springs. It's the truck. I know it is."

Tate held up a hand to slow her down. "All right. What else?"

"Second, one thumbprint from the truck bed belongs to Nolan Parris."

"The priest?"

Estelle nodded. "It was on the outside, consistent with gripping the truck side while standing on the ground. We have no evidence that shows he was actually up in the truck bed."

"I'll be damned," Tate muttered. "What would he have to do with all this?"

"He's the father of Cecila Burgess's daughter."

Tate ducked his head with surprise. "You shitting me?"

"No."

Tate looked at me. "Is this the kid you told me about

last night? The one who's staying with the hippies at the hot springs?"

"Yes."

"And the priest is the father? You didn't tell me that part."

I was about to say something like there were lots of things I didn't tell lots of people, but Estelle saved me from my tired temper. "That was an angle we were just starting to work on when Paul found the truck."

Tate crushed out one cigarette and lit another that he bummed from Al Martinez. "So what's the connection?"

When he said that, every pair of eyes in the room was locked on Estelle. They were expecting a grand pronouncement, I guess.

"I don't know," she said.

Tate held up his hands, prompting. "Is Parris a suspect? In your mind? Did he kill the girl?"

Estelle shook her head immediately. "No. That doesn't make any sense."

"Did he kill the two young men up on the mesa? Revenge, maybe?"

"We thought about that," Estelle said and looked at me. "I'm not sure he's capable of it. And you, sir?"

"Stranger things have happened." I was no longer so eager to make assumptions.

"You're going to talk with him today?" Tate asked.

"Yes, sir."

The sheriff took a deep breath and looked around for a chair. "We're going to have to get you some furniture." He settled for sucking in his gut and sliding his hands down behind his belt, like he had gas. If he ate at Bobby's too many more times, he would. "I need to go back to the city, or I'd go with you. Bill, are you staying with us for a while?"

I shrugged. "I'm kinda curious now. Besides, I need about thirty-six hours of sleep before I tackle an eight-hour drive home."

"All right. Estelle, I'm leaving both Paul Garcia and Al Martinez here. Whatever you need, holler."

Estelle nodded. "If we keep this kind of quiet for a while, it might be easier," she said. "If the killer is still in the county, I'd rather not spook him."

"In that you're lucky," Tate said. "If this was the city, you'd have thirty-five media types crawling down your neck. Hell, nobody outside of San Estevan knows we're here unless we tell 'em." He stood up. "Go talk to the priest who's strayed into fatherhood and let me know." He grinned at his own dumb joke, then turned to the two deputies. "Paul and Al, are you all set? Anything you need?"

Both shook their heads, and Tate prompted Martinez by adding, "Give your wife a call, Al. Tell her you'll probably be home tomorrow. Maybe Tuesday."

He picked up his baseball cap and snugged it down on his head. "It's my granddaughter's birthday today, and I'll be at my son's house most of the afternoon if you need me. The dispatcher will know. Bill, you take care. Don't push so hard. You look like hell." Tate thrust out his jaw like a master sergeant who's just given his troops their marching orders and was now going to retire back to the comfort of his quarters.

"Thanks," I said. "That's going to be my epitaph."

ESTELLE SENT DEPUTY Martinez north to orbit Quebrada Mesa. Paul Garcia pulled a sleeping bag out of his Suburban and spread it out on the office floor. "Wonderful," he said and was asleep in ten seconds at most.

I envied that kind of metabolism. But what the hell. I'd had insomnia for so long I had developed the skill of falling asleep with my eyes open, in the middle of a conversation. If I actually were to lie down to rest, I'd end up staring at the ceiling.

Estelle ran on her own private, inexhaustible power pack. Her ancient mother would have had biting words to say about her daughter's apparent disregard for her own *condicion*, but I knew better than to say anything. I knew damn well that the hours were going to catch up with both of us, sooner rather than later.

As we drove out of the highway department yard, Estelle glanced at her watch. "It's almost ten. Do you think we'll catch Parris between services?"

"Maybe. Or you might wait until later this afternoon. Catch yourself a few hours rest."

"I'm not tired."

I stretched and groaned. "I bet." I could see the determination set into the muscles of her face. "Estelle, trust me. Parris isn't going anywhere. And if he makes a break, a radio's faster."

"That's not what worries me."

"Yeah, I know it isn't. Daisy's been up there with H. T. Finn for a couple of days. She's enjoying the hell out of life in the woods. Her father knows she's there. It's a beautiful day. It isn't going to rain and give anyone pneumonia." I looked over at her. "Your mothering instinct is in overdrive."

"Do you want to go home?"

"To Posadas? No. I want you to get some rest so you don't make a mistake that you'll regret. And yes, I want some rest. If we go and see Parris, the next thing you'll want to do is walk up to the hot springs again." I shook my head. "The old snowball effect is going to get you."

Estelle looked like she wanted to say something, to argue. But old habits are hard to break. She knew I didn't lean on her unless there was a reason.

"Look at it this way," I said. "Al Martinez seems bright enough. He's got his eyes open. And every road up there is covered, either by the Forest Service or some of the sheriff's department reservists that Tate called in."

She gave in finally and told the dispatcher that we would be ten-seven.

We heard: "Four-o-six, do you copy?" Al Martinez acknowledged. We reached the adobe, and Francis Guzman's Isuzu was in the driveway. I stepped out and level ground felt good. What felt even better was the cool, dark interior of the adobe.

Estelle walked quietly to the bedroom, looked inside, and then turned to me, holding her hands up on her cheek, like a kid sleeping. Francis was home and zonked. She showed me the tiny guest room—about the size of an Amtrak sleeping berth.

"Don't go anywhere without letting me know," I ordered, and Estelle grinned.

"No, sir."

Then I surprised myself. My head hit the pillow, my nose enjoyed the faint aroma of clean cotton for a few seconds, and I fell asleep. My dreams were a restless jumble at first, but then I dreamed that Nolan Parris was helping Daisy Burgess build stinkbug traps.

# SIXTEEN

I SLEPT SOUNDLY until about four that afternoon. A car door slammed and I opened one eye and looked at my watch. Other than that I didn't move.

What the hell. Nothing was going to happen up on Quebrada Mesa. That sorry patch of ground was sealed tight. Sheriff Tate's staff had notified the victims' next of kin. The medical examiner in the city would release the bodies to the families when every last *t* was crossed and *i* dotted. And Estelle didn't need to worry about Nolan Parris…he wasn't going anywhere.

I stretched and found a new ache. In the distance I heard a telephone ring and then quiet voices. I rolled onto my back and covered my eyes with one arm. Maybe we'd have a quiet dinner and go to bed early. We'd see Parris in the morning.

By then the Social Services office would be open and Estelle could turn Daisy's case over to them if Parris balked about custody. That sounded pretty good. I enjoyed the illusion for another two minutes.

At six minutes after four a knuckle rapped on my bedroom door.

"Yo!" I called. I put my hand behind my neck and raised my head a little.

The door opened and Estelle looked in. I was surprised to see she was in uniform. "What's up?"

"There's been a hunting accident over on the west

side of the pueblo. The pueblo police asked us to assist. You want to come?"

"Sure," I answered with more enthusiasm than I felt. I swung my feet off the bed and pulled on my boots, shoved the clip of the slip-on holster over my belt, and wondered for a minute where the hell I'd put my hat. I got up and walked out into the living room.

"Here," Estelle said, holding the Stetson out to me.

"This means no dinner again, doesn't it?"

"We'll catch something," she said cheerfully. "Anyway, we won't be long. It's not our case. We're just assisting Buddy Vallo."

I got into the car and noticed that Francis Guzman's Isuzu was gone.

"Is Francis already out there?" Estelle nodded.

"Who was it? Do you know?"

"No. Paul Garcia called dispatch and asked for me. That's all I know."

"You get tangled up in reservation jurisdiction, and you'll be there forever," I muttered.

"Well, they have only two officers," Estelle said. "Buddy is chief…he's Mary Vallo's husband…Francis's nurse? And Buddy has one assistant who works nights. Sometimes that's not enough." I didn't bother to remind her that there was only one of her for the entire northwest end of the county.

We skirted what looked like the main residential area of Isidro Pueblo. There wasn't an extra square inch of packed dust to spare. Low, brown adobes that had been settling into the hard earth for centuries lined the single-track roadway.

Estelle slowed down. There were lots of children

and they watched us go by with eyes wide. We headed for the river.

The crossing was one of those upside-down bridges where the engineers make a concrete dip through the riverbed. When the river is rolling, nobody crosses. It's that simple. I could have jumped across the trickle of water that day.

The road turned south, following the river for a quarter of a mile before turning west again around a series of rolling hills that formed the base of Chuparrosa Mesa.

I relaxed as we poked along at forty miles an hour on a road designed for ten. The road forked again, one path going up through the hills. Estelle took the other, keeping to the flatland. We angled away from the river toward the vast, open country that stretched virtually unblemished to the Arizona border. The patrol car crested an abrupt rise and bounced down hard enough to scrape the undercarriage.

The road ran along the rim of a deep arroyo, and up ahead I saw Guzman's Isuzu, Paul Garcia's Suburban, and a white Chevy Blazer with government plates. Well off the road, its wheels less than a yard from the arroyo edge, was another vehicle, an old and battered International Scout.

We slid to a stop. So deep was this erosion cut that I couldn't see the bottom until I stepped out of the car. Fifty yards up the arroyo I saw the officers. Estelle's hand-held radio crackled.

"Estelle, there's a spot behind you guys where you can get down into the arroyo. If you walk up the far side, you won't disturb anything."

Estelle waved a hand. We found where both Paul,

Francis, and the Indian cop had slid down through the loose sand, and we followed their tracks up the arroyo bed.

The body was lying facedown, close to the arroyo side, with fresh sand from the edge both under and on top of the corpse. He was an Indian, maybe eighteen or twenty, broad-shouldered, and husky bordering on fat.

Estelle stood on the opposite side of the arroyo and looked first at the body, then at the area. I know she would have preferred that everyone had stayed well away until she had arrived, but the damage had been done. The Indian policeman watched us but made no move to walk over to meet us.

"Hello, Buddy," Estelle called, and he nodded a greeting. He was of indeterminate age, moon-faced, and short. My first impression was one of great patience. I guess he'd have to be patient, working law enforcement in an area the size of an average cattle ranch. I'd have been bored to pudding in a month. He stood with his hands in his pockets, leaning against the arroyo bank, watching the doctor.

Francis Guzman knelt just beyond the corpse's feet, waiting for Estelle's undivided attention.

"What killed him?" I asked, walking across the arroyo.

"A single gunshot wound under the chin," Guzman said. When he saw Estelle step closer, he stood up and gently pulled the corpse's shoulder, rolling the body just enough so that we could see the weapon underneath. It was one of those stubby little .22 autoloaders.

"See the hand?" Francis asked. The man's index finger was still in the trigger guard and was twisted awkwardly.

When the victim had fallen, he'd clenched onto that rifle out of reflex. He'd have been better off to drop it. Sometime during the fall, probably when he'd crashed to the arroyo bottom, he'd jerked the trigger.

The small bullet had torn into his throat on the right side of the Adam's apple. He'd bled profusely from the mouth, and Guzman added, "It angled up...almost straight up. Through the roof of his mouth and into the brain."

"It looks like he fell when the edge of the arroyo caved in," Estelle said.

"That's what I guessed," Buddy said. I squinted at his name tag and read Rupert Vallo.

"Who called it in?"

"I found him myself," Paul Garcia said. He was on quite a roll.

Estelle looked sharply at him. "What were you doing over here?" When she said that, the corner of Buddy Vallo's mouth twitched just a little. Indian pueblos were sovereign, each with its own police department. We were careful not to trespass on their turf unless asked. Their lead agency for the serious stuff was the Federal Bureau of Investigation—and who the hell wanted to mess with *their* paperwork.

Garcia said, "I left the station and was going to patrol south, since Deputy Martinez was up on the mesa. One of the things on my list was to talk with Chief Vallo here and find out what I could about Robert Waquie. Maybe find out who he hung around with. Maybe get a lead on who was with him Friday night in the truck."

He took a breath and continued as if he were reading from a report.

"Then I heard on the scanner that the Forest Service had a little brush fire off to the west somewhere. They were reporting smoke but hadn't found the source yet. And you know how they've been talkin' that one little smoker could spread and take out the whole mountain. So I thought, what the hell. I was already headed this way.

"I got to the pueblo and saw that this dirt road crossed the river. So I decided to follow it and see if it went far enough to reach the National Forest over on the mesa. Maybe I could see the smoke better from over here. Three point two miles later, I see this Scout parked by the road. Just out of habit, I checked the plate. I saw that the tag was expired so I called it in. Then I got out to look around." He shrugged.

"That's when I saw the fresh crumbled sand along the arroyo lip. I got to lookin', went downstream a ways, and then I saw him."

"How'd the plate come back?"

"The Scout's registered to a Cecil Lucero. From here."

"That's Cecil," Buddy Vallo said. "I know him real good." A long pause followed. "I warned him about the license plate last week. Him and Robert Waquie, I spend more time chasin' their tails than anybody else in the pueblo."

Estelle glanced at Vallo. I saw a flicker of what might have been annoyance. She knelt down as Francis handed her the man's wallet. The corpse's driver's license said that Cecil Lucero had turned twenty-one three days before.

"Are there any other injuries?" I asked Francis.

"A broken index finger on his right hand."

"Caught in the trigger guard when he fell?" Estelle asked.

Francis nodded. "Probably."

"How long's he been here?"

"I'm no expert on postmortem lividity," Francis said, "but if I had to guess, I'd say no more than a couple hours…five or six at the outside."

Estelle straightened up and craned her neck to see the top of the arroyo. The sides were steep and twelve feet high…enough that we couldn't see the truck unless we stepped to nearly the center of the arroyo.

More to herself than any of us, she said, "So he maybe saw a rabbit or something, stopped, got out, and got excited. Stepped too close. The arroyo is a little undercut here. It caved in and he fell. Pop."

"That's what I thought," Paul Garcia said.

"I don't see any other obvious tracks," I said. The bottom of the arroyo was a mass of hoofprints where rambling cattle had mixed the gravelly sand.

"Did you see any tracks when you climbed down here?" Estelle asked Buddy Vallo.

"No."

She looked at Paul Garcia. "And he was dead when you found him?"

"Yes. He sure was."

Estelle methodically pressed on. "Was the Scout idling when you came by or switched off?"

"Off. The keys were in the ignition."

"And the driver's door was closed?"

"Yes."

"And the window?"

"Closed."

"Was the door locked?"

"I didn't check."

Estelle frowned. I said to Estelle, "You're wondering about the window, aren't you?"

"That's what I was wondering."

"People do drive with their windows closed, Estelle."

"When it's ninety out and they're hunting?"

I exhaled wearily. "Estelle, maybe he was planning to do some hiking. He got out and buttoned the thing up."

"Then he locked his keys in the car."

"That's happened before."

We heard another vehicle and Francis Guzman said, "That's probably the ambulance. One unit was tied up with a transfer, and they had to get the second one out of the garage."

Estelle turned to her briefcase and began to unpack the camera equipment. She was still frowning and thinking hard, and I knew it was best just to let her stew until she was ready to put the pieces together.

But this time if she was trying to tie Lucero's accident to the murders up on Quebrada Mesa, she was daydreaming. She had the murder jitters. Vallo had mentioned Lucero and Waquie in the same breath, but what the hell did that mean? The pueblo was tiny. The odds were nearly a hundred percent that two victims from the same village would know each other.

What had happened here was obvious to me. Accidents where the hunter shot himself almost always involved a fence, a fall, or a dropped weapon...one or more of the three. This one fit the pattern.

I looked around for some shade. Even in the late afternoon, the arroyo was an oven. It was going to stay that way until sunset, too, since the arroyo's general orientation was east-west. And when Estelle began her unpacking, I knew I had time to spare.

My bladder began to send signals. The only tree in sight was a sorry little scrub juniper that was about to fall out of the arroyo bank fifty yards upstream. At that point, the arroyo veered to the right.

"I'm going around the corner," I said and thrust my hands in my pockets as I walked slowly through the soft sand. It was almost as much work as trudging up a mountainside.

I reached the juniper and stopped. What looked like a single boot print was pressed into the sand. It was hard to be sure, since the sand was so coarse and dry that it refused to hold any positive definition. I stood and looked at the mark, then up at the slope where the juniper was hanging on.

If someone wanted to climb up out of the arroyo, this was a good spot. The bank was sloped, and cattle had beaten an obvious trail down from the top.

With the lack of rain the boot print—if indeed it was one—could have been made any time in the past month. I decided to walk around the next "S" in the arroyo for some privacy. I took about twenty steps.

"Well, son of a bitch," I said aloud and stopped in my tracks. My right hand drifted around behind my back to where the stubby .357 nestled. I didn't move for a good three minutes, looking and listening.

With my hand still on the magnum, I stepped forward to take a closer look at the corpse. No hunting accident had dropped this one.

# SEVENTEEN

THE CORPSE LAY on his face, arms and legs outstretched like he'd been bashed to the ground by a giant club.

A bloodstain the size of a dinner plate soaked his denim work shirt. The shirt was old and faded, with plenty of rips here and there, the kind barbed wire would tear when a man's a little careless ducking through fences.

I stepped closer. The seven small holes in the center of his back weren't from barbs…and they were grouped tightly enough that I could have covered them with my hand.

Without moving my feet I twisted around looking for spent shell casings. There were none. I walked backward the way I had come, trying not to disturb the arroyo bottom. A half dozen times I thought I had found a shell casing, but it was only the sun winking from the quartz-loaded stream gravel.

At the juniper I turned around. Downsteam, the ambulance crew was just making preparations to load Cecil Lucero's body on the gurney. I whistled sharply. Estelle Reyes-Guzman must have read the urgency on my face, because she got off her knees where she'd been photographing the .22 rifle and walked up the arroyo to meet me.

"I don't think this is a simple hunting accident," I said.

"Why? What did you find?"

"There's another corpse, just around the corner. And he didn't fall on his own gun."

"Shot?"

"Yes."

"For sure murder?"

"No doubt. Seven times in the back. That's tough to do by accident."

"Son of a bitch," Estelle breathed. It was the first time I'd ever heard her curse. She touched my elbow. "Lead me up there. I'll walk in your tracks."

"THAT'S KENNETH LUCERO," Buddy Vallo said.

"Cecil's brother?" Estelle asked.

Vallo nodded. "Younger brother." Buddy pointed, holding his arm out straight like he was pointing a rifle. "You can see their truck from here."

I stepped over to where he was standing, just where the arroyo turned south. Sure enough, for several feet the banks didn't block the view.

"Maybe seventy yards," I said. "Any kid with a scoped rifle could do that or better." I looked at Estelle. "Hell, even I could shoot like that."

Francis Guzman pulled up Kenneth Lucero's shirt. The bullet holes were small and dimpled inward. "Right through the spine, at heart level," Francis said, pointing at two of the small holes.

"That explains why he dropped in a heap," I said. "Just like tagging a rabbit in midhop." I knelt down. "Twenty-two caliber, you think?"

Guzman nodded. "Not much bleeding. No through-and-through. That's what I would guess."

"And the rifle downstream is a semiautomatic," I said.

"There's still one bullet in the clip of the rifle and one in the chamber," Estelle said. "The clip's capacity is ten." She turned to Buddy Vallo. "It could have happened that way. Cecil could have shot his brother and then fell and shot himself by accident. That would account for all the rounds."

"If the gun was fully loaded in the first place," I reminded her. She squinted against the sun and harsh sand. "We need to find those shell casings."

I asked Vallo, "Was there any animosity between the two brothers? Anything that might have led to this?"

He pushed out his lower lip and frowned. "Maybe. Brothers fight sometimes." I was about to add that a fight between siblings usually didn't result in murder, but Vallo added, "And they were both chasin' the same girl."

He half grinned at the irony of it. "I don't think she was interested in either one of 'em. She was a white girl." He said it as if that explained everything. He hadn't spent much time in society outside Isidro Pueblo, where you never could be sure who—or even what—was going to experiment with matrimony.

Estelle asked, "Who's the girl?"

"Lucy Grider. She lives on that ranch on the way to Encinas."

"Where the hell is that?" I asked. The girl's name hadn't registered.

"About six miles. Where the state road forks, south of the pueblo? You go east. It's a little village up that valley. She's the sister to one of the boys you pulled off the mesa yesterday."

I turned and looked with surprise at Estelle. She'd sat down abruptly on a hummock of sand. She took off her Stetson and dropped it crown down beside her. "Kelly Grider's sister," she said. "I don't believe this." She looked up at me. "Waquie and Grider were killed together. Now these two. They both chased Grider's sister."

"They hung out together off and on," Vallo said. "The four of them?"

"I've seen them together."

"I would have liked to have known that," Estelle said, more to herself than anyone else. But she knew as well as I that the information would have come out in due time. None of us had been at leisure the past thirty-six hours to survey the county, picking up leads. "Have you seen anyone else with them?" Estelle asked, and Vallo shook his head. Old man Waquie had said five in the truck…maybe he'd miscounted. Or maybe the fifth one had been Cecilia Burgess.

Estelle took a deep breath. "All right. We've got the daylight. I want this arroyo swept clean. I want those shell casings. And anything else. Paul, go back the way we came, start at the truck, and, really carefully, work along the top edge of the arroyo to this spot and even beyond. Then do the same on the other side, just in case. Buddy and I will work the body and this area."

She turned to me. "Sir, would you dust Lucero's truck? The print kit is in the trunk of the car."

"You bet. Are you going to call Pat Tate?"

"After a bit. We're on the reservation, and it's Buddy's case. It's up to him." She raised an eyebrow at Vallo.

"Let's see what we find," he said. "Maybe this is as far as it goes."

Stranger things had happened, of course. But I think the same scenario was going through my mind as Estelle's. That little International Scout was small enough that a man could hide it pretty easily...especially on a mesa as thickly timbered as Quebrada Mesa. And if there'd been friction between the Luceros and Grider over the latter's sister, who the hell knew.

If Cecil Lucero was cold-blooded enough to use his own brother for target practice, he'd have had no trouble arranging a trip for two friends over a cliff—and then snapping a neck afterward.

# EIGHTEEN

LUCY GRIDER MIGHT have been able to provide some answers. I was surprised when Estelle sent Paul Garcia to Encinas to interview her. I had to agree that Paul was as diligent a rookie as I'd ever seen—it was hard to be irritated at him for chasing brushfire smoke when, in the process, he'd stumbled onto a murder.

Estelle coached him on what questions to ask and then we headed home shortly after eight that evening. This snowball of events was leaving us miles behind in its wake.

"I want to talk with Nolan Parris," she said as we turned into the dirt lane that led to the Guzman adobe. "And I want to talk with him tonight."

I should have guessed that was coming. She pulled into her driveway and asked, "Will you go with me?"

"Of course," I said. "If you feed me first." Francis pulled into the driveway before we reached the front step. He hadn't slammed the Isuzu's door before Estelle met him. The two kids embraced for a long time.

"Seems like a couple of days since I've seen you," she said, and Francis laughed and removed her Stetson so the brim wouldn't hit him in the mouth when she hugged him. Their nap that afternoon had done some good.

"You don't like clandestine meetings out in hidden arroyos?" he asked. I went inside so they'd have a minute together without a chaperone. I tossed my hat on the two-cushion sofa and pulled the holstered revolver off my belt.

The telephone was on the wall by the doorway to the kitchen. I dialed zero and then Martin Holman's home number in Posadas. The call went through after I gave the mechanical-sounding operator the billing. It rang twice, and then another robotic voice said, "I'm sorry, that number is temporarily out of service. If you need assistance, please stay on the line and an operator will help you." I hung up, perplexed. Holman didn't earn a bundle as sheriff of Posadas County, but he sure as hell earned enough to pay his phone bill. Maybe his four-year-old had jerked the cord out of the wall. The little bastard was capable of that and worse.

Estelle and Francis came in the house just as I was dialing the Posadas County Sheriff's Department. Gayle Sedillos was working the desk. She was the best dispatcher we had. Estelle had started that way. But unlike Estelle, Gayle had no aspirations beyond the desk. She answered the phone after the first ring.

"Where's Holman?" I asked the instant she said she'd accept the call.

"He hasn't gotten hold of you, sir?"

"No. What's he want?" Holman always wanted something, and most of the time it could wait.

There was a pause at the other end, and I could hear voices. Then Gayle said, "Sir, Bob Torrez just came in. Let me have you talk with him."

I glanced at Estelle and looked heavenward. She grinned.

Deputy Bob Torrez picked up the phone. His voice was usually so soft I had a hard time hearing him.

"Sir?"

"What's up, Bob?"

"Sheriff Holman was trying to get hold of you earlier today," Torrez said.

I glanced down at the unchecked answering machine where his message no doubt awaited. "We were out," I said. "What's he want?"

"His house burned down last night."

"His house burned down?"

"Yes, sir."

"Anyone hurt?"

"No, sir. But the house was a complete loss. And his two dogs."

"How'd the fire happen?"

"We don't know, sir. But we've sealed the place off. The sheriff's out there. And the investigators from the fire department are still out there."

"Are they going to need an assist?" Sheriff Holman had lived in the village of Posadas and the volunteer fire department was eager and generally efficient. But the two men who called themselves investigators were good-intentioned amateurs.

"They haven't said," Torrez answered.

"Call the state office and get somebody over from Cruces," I suggested. "And you're sure everyone's all right?"

"Yes, sir. Sheriff Holman sent the family to Deming to stay with relatives. And he's staying at the Essex Motel."

I groaned. "Christ, nobody wants to live in a motel, Bob. Holman knows where the key to my house is. Tell him to use it."

"I'll pass the message along, sir. He wanted to know when you were planning to head home."

"It's going to be a day or two. We've got a little action up here, and I'm giving Estelle the benefit of my vast wisdom."

Torrez took that seriously as he did most things. "Yes, sir. Sheriff Holman wanted to know if you were coming back tomorrow."

"I'll see. It's unlikely though. Just tell him to use my house and call the state fire marshal's office, if he hasn't already."

"Yes, sir."

"Let me talk with Gayle now."

"Yes, sir."

When the dispatcher came on the phone, I said, "Gayle, is there anything the Holmans need that you know of?"

"I don't think so, sir. But I'll ask. They sure lost everything, though."

"Well, tell him to use my house instead of camping out at the damn motel."

"I'll do that. How's Estelle doing?"

"Fine. You want to talk with her?" She said yes, and I held the phone out to Estelle. They talked for ten minutes. Maybe Holman would have enough on his mind that he wouldn't rant about the phone bill.

Estelle finally hung up and for the first time since I'd set foot in San Estevan, the three of us had dinner together.

I damn near drooled a puddle as I watched the enchiladas sink in a sea of fresh green chili. Francis handed me what I hoped would be the first of several cold beers. He poured a glass of red wine for Estelle. Estelle must have read something on my face, because she said, "Vitamin W. It goes with Mexican food better than that stuff you guys drink."

The fire of her chili was undiminished…it made even the cafe's burrito grande seem like a bland milk shake. I wiped my forehead, blew my nose, and panted. "God, this is good. Destructive, but good."

"Destructive, hell," Francis said. "Did you know it's been proven in the lab that green chili kills bacteria?"

"I don't doubt it," I said. "Does the kid start kicking when you eat this stuff?"

Estelle laughed. "Not at two months, sir."

"What are you going to name him?"

"Or her," Francis said and handed me another beer. "Ask me again in seven months," Estelle replied.

"Is your mother going to come up here?"

"For the grand event, you mean?" Estelle shook her head. "We're going to Tres Santos."

"You're kidding."

"They've got a pretty good clinic there," Francis said.

I frowned and said, "Huh," for want of anything better.

"My mother is too frail to travel up here," Estelle said. "This probably will be the only grandchild she lives to meet. There are worse things than being born in that big adobe house in Mexico."

"Huh," I said again. I shrugged. "What do the Guzmans think of that idea?"

"They're going to be there, too."

Estelle offered seconds and like a fool I accepted. "El Padrino should be present, too," she said.

"I'm flattered. But I've had so many days off that

Holman's not going to let me take another one for five years."

"Are you going back tomorrow?"

"Probably I should." I glanced at my watch. It was night shift time again. "You'll wrap this up this evening, after we talk with Parris....I'm interested in what he has to say about his prints being on the truck."

"Do you think that Cecil Lucero shot his brother?"

"Don't you?"

She toyed with the remains of the enchilada on her plate. "I don't know. Usually, when I'm sure of how something happened, I can picture it in my mind."

"The two of them got out of the Scout and walked a ways up along the arroyo," Francis said. "Kenneth went down into the arroyo. Cecil shot him from up above."

"Maybe."

"That's where Paul found the seven shell casings this afternoon, Estelle," I said.

"The M.E. will tell you for sure about the angle of the bullets," Francis said. "After the shooting, Cecil walks back toward the Scout. He's nervous. So like most of us would, he turns around to look back up the arroyo. He can't see his brother's body, so he steps closer to the edge to try another view." He shrugged.

"What's the problem with that?" I asked.

"I'd feel better if we'd found the last casing," Estelle said. "I'd feel better if I had that."

"There are any number of ways it could have happened that make sense," I said. Estelle nodded, but I knew she wasn't convinced. I pushed my plate away and stood up. I said what she really wanted to hear. "Let's go see Parris."

# NINETEEN

---

FATHER NOLAN PARRIS greeted us at the door, and it seemed as if he had expected us—and more than that… he was somehow relieved we'd returned.

"I think you know Deputy Reyes-Guzman?" I said as Parris showed us into the front room.

"Our paths have crossed once or twice," Parris said. He and Estelle shook hands. "Would you folks like some coffee or tea or something?"

We declined, and Parris closed the door. His limp hadn't improved. He gestured to chairs and we sat. Estelle pulled out her notebook and pen and said, "Father Parris, I want to talk with you about Friday night."

Parris nodded and folded his hands, waiting.

Estelle leafed through the notebook, stopping to read here and there. "Father, as you may have heard, we're investigating the deaths of two young men. Their truck somehow went over the edge of Quebrada Mesa, probably sometime early yesterday evening."

Parris again nodded. "A tragic thing," he said quietly.

"Father, we have reason to believe that the truck in question was also involved somehow in the death of Cecilia Burgess on Friday night."

Parris sat back in the chair. His right hand drifted up to touch his pectoral cross. He watched Estelle. It may have been my imagination, but I sensed an inner calm that hadn't been there the day before.

Estelle looked up from her notes and cocked her head, giving Parris an opportunity. The priest held up his left hand, palm up, as if he were going to beckon for more information. His right hand remained on the cross. "And you feel that I have information about that night?"

"Yes, sir, I do."

Parris looked at me. "Since we talked yesterday, I've had time for considerable counsel." I didn't ask if it was counsel with someone else or with his own soul. It didn't matter as long as he had the right answers.

Nolan Parris took a deep breath, held it, and then released it the way a smoker might jet out a long, thin plume of smoke.

"On Friday evening I was out in the garden. Perhaps you've seen it, beyond the driveway. It's not far from the highway. I'm not a gardener but it's a quiet spot for reflection. There's an old wooden bench under one of the apricot trees that's a favorite of mine. I like to sit there and watch the stars.

"Anyway, shortly after ten…in fact, I was just about to go inside…I glanced up as several cars passed. In the light of their headlights I noticed Cecilia Burgess. She was walking along the highway."

"Northbound?" I asked.

"Yes. But on the other side of the highway, facing traffic." He hesitated. "I saw the moment as an opportunity, I suppose. I called to her. Now you must understand that we haven't been on the best of terms… at least from her point of view. I thought that she was going to ignore me and so I called again. She crossed

the highway. I wanted to talk with her about Daisy...
about where the child might go to preschool in the fall,
where the two of them were planning to stay. I was uneasy that she might not have made plans."

"Were you able to settle anything?" Estelle asked.

Parris shook his head. "No. In fact, I made matters worse, I suppose. She asked me how much I was
willing to pay, and I hesitated. She interpreted that as
reluctance on my part to provide for the child. I tried
to explain to her that I simply have no funds of my
own—nothing significant anyway. She didn't accept
that. I tried to explain that there might be some sort
of diocesan help...scholarships, housing, maybe that
sort of thing. She took offense at that, perhaps thinking that I wanted the child in someone else's custody
other than her own."

"Did you?" I asked.

"No, of course not. A child should be with its mother
if at all possible. But Cecilia became angry. We'd had
this same conversation before, I suppose. I tried to reason with her, and she became angrier still. She could
be a most vocal young woman." Parris looked rueful.
"As her voice raised, I tried to calm her, and that made
her even angrier."

He held up both hands. "I'm afraid I made a stupid
mistake. Thinking that she might react positively to a
show of strength on my part, I reached out and held her
by the elbow. I told her that if she really cared about
the child, she wouldn't leave Daisy out in the forest
while she walks here and there late at night along a
busy highway.

"I offered to drive her up to the hot springs. She
retorted that I was last person she wanted to be seen

with and that she'd walk wherever and whenever she pleased." Parris shrugged. "It was one of those verbal fights that just…well, nobody wins."

Estelle asked, "Did it end there?"

"No," Parris said. "By this time, we had moved from the garden where I'd first suggested that we talk out to the shoulder of the highway. There were several on-coming cars, and as if to spite me, she stuck out her thumb to hitch a ride. None of the traffic stopped, of course." He looked down. "I wanted nothing more than to jump into the underbrush along the road and hide." He looked at me and smiled slightly. "I'm not much of a hero, am I?"

An appropriate philosophical reply didn't material-ize in my head, so I just shrugged.

Parris looked pained. "The next vehicle came around the corner almost immediately, and it did stop. It was the Ford pickup truck. I don't think I've ever felt such panic because I could see, perfectly clearly, what would happen." He stopped and both hands clutched the crucifix.

"A blue and white truck?" Estelle asked.

"Yes. I've seen it in the neighborhood on a number of occasions."

"How many occupants?"

"There were at least four. Maybe five." He hesitated. "Let me think." After a moment he said, "Five. Two in the bed and three up in the cab. I knew from their behavior that they had been drinking."

"What did they do?"

"They were loud and when the two in the back stood up to see why the truck had stopped, they could hardly keep their balance. The passenger on the window side held out a can toward Cecilia."

"And she accepted a ride from them," Estelle said, and I could see that she had finished the story for herself.

"I tried to prevent it; I really did. Cecilia stepped up on the back bumper, then over the tailgate, before I could reach her. She almost lost her balance, but one of the drunks helped her to the front of the truck bed. I reached the side of the truck and grabbed ahold, pleading with her to show some sense. The driver stepped on the gas hard just as one of them pushed me away. I thought for a moment I was going to be hit by the rear tire."

"That's when you sprained your ankle?" I asked, but Parris shook his head.

"No. They drove off, and I could see the truck weave this way and that. I was furious with myself and petrified for Cecilia. I pictured every tragedy that might happen except the one that did.

"I pictured the truck weaving off the highway and into the river. Or crashing head-on into someone else. The more I thought about it the worse I felt.

"Finally the obvious solution was the easiest one. I took the retreat's station wagon and drove up the highway. I reached the campground and stopped. If they had let Cecilia off there, she would be walking up the trail to Finn's campsite. So I parked and tried to find the trail. My flashlight wasn't very good, but eventually I found the path and the Forest Service signs."

I reflected that while Parris was stumbling around among the ponderosas, I had been snoring away in the Blazer, right there in the parking lot. He would have had to walk within a dozen paces of me. That was another reason to give up on the damn exercise routine. If I hadn't taken the hike earlier, I would probably have been lying in the Blazer, eyes open like a lemur, insomnia in control. I'd missed a chance.

"I found the camp," Parris said. "And Cecilia wasn't there. Both Finn and the boy who stays with him were. Finn told me that Daisy was asleep in the tent. I told him what had happened."

"What was his reaction?" Estelle asked.

"I'm not sure. It was dark and other than the campfire and my flashlight, there wasn't much light to see by. He told me that she probably was up the canyon, maybe at one of the other campgrounds, partying…that she'd be all right…that she could take care of herself."

"Did you give Finn a description of the truck?"

Parris frowned. "Not a description. Not like you would. But I told him who I thought it was."

"Who do you think owns the truck?" I asked.

"I don't know who owns it. But I've seen one of the Waquie boys driving it on occasion. And his father. The family are parish members."

"And you mentioned the name to Finn?" Estelle asked.

"Yes."

"Then what?"

"Finn offered me a cup of coffee. He had a pot on the fire."

"That's it?"

"Yes."

"You didn't discuss Daisy with him?" I asked.

"No. I have to admit, Sheriff, that Finn makes me uneasy. Cecilia had mentioned at one time that Finn

was a minister of some sort. I've only met him twice—
that night was the second time. Both times, he looked at
me…and my Roman collar…as if I were something of
a joke." Parris managed a wan smile. "I know I've got
an active imagination. But that's the impression I got."

He looked up at the ceiling, using a dramatic pause
like a good storyteller does when he's organizing his
thoughts.

"But I found myself thinking that if I accepted a
cup of coffee, that might somehow bring the two of
us—Finn and me—a little closer, and I'd be able to
talk with him."

"But that wasn't the case," I said.

"No. In fact, he handed me the cup and then went
into the tent. So did the boy. Without a word. I stayed
by the fire a few minutes, and when it was obvious that
our conversation was over I left. Just a moment or two
after the boy did."

"Arajanian left?"

"Is that his name? Yes. He and Finn talked a little
when they came out of the tent, and then the boy left.
He went down the hill. Finn went back in the tent."

"You didn't go with him?"

Parris shook his head. "No. And I could never have
kept up with him anyway. He ran." Parris shook his
head. "Like a ghost. He didn't even use a light."

I could feel Estelle looking at me and when I glanced
at her, I could see that her face was set like stone.

When she spoke, her voice was so low I could hardly
hear her. "When you left, Finn was still in camp?"

Parris nodded.

"And then you walked back to your station wagon
in the campground."

"Yes. It took me nearly an hour. I fell hard, just above the fork in the trail. I thought I had broken my ankle." He rubbed his sock. "But it's just a bad sprain."

"And then you drove back here," Estelle asked. "What did you do between that time and when you heard about Cecilia?"

"Prayed, I suppose," Parris said. He looked at me thoughtfully.

"I lied to you earlier, Sheriff. I told you I found out about Cecilia the next morning at Garcia's Trading Post. That's not the case."

He turned to Estelle as if he wanted to make sure she got it right in her notes. "I heard all the sirens. I'm sure everyone in the valley did. I knew right away that whatever it was, the emergency somehow involved Cecilia. I knew it in my heart. I got up, got dressed, and took the station wagon."

"With that bad ankle?"

"Yes. And I drove north until I came to the accident site. I saw all the red lights, the ambulance…I saw that they were just loading the gurney. I'm ashamed to say that I rationalized myself out of it at that point."

"Meaning what?" I asked.

"Meaning that I should have stopped. I saw her face, knew it was her. I should have talked with you on the spot. But I decided that I couldn't help Cecilia any more just then. She was in good hands. There was nothing I could do. So I drove back to the retreat, and when I learned she'd been transferred to the city, I drove to Albuquerque."

"And you were at the hospital when she died?"

"Yes. The rest of my story, as I told you yesterday, is the truth."

"Did you ever have your ankle looked at by a physician?"

"No."

"Why not?" I asked.

"It's just a bad sprain. There's nothing a doctor could do for it that I can't."

"Did anyone else here at the retreat look at it?"

Parris frowned at my question. "Well, yes. Father Sandoval examined it shortly after I returned home. I had planned to ask him to look at it in the morning, but apparently he'd been awakened by the station wagon pulling into the driveway. He said he looked out the window and saw me limp to the front steps." Parris turned and gestured at the door. "He met me in the entranceway and insisted that he look at the ankle then and there."

"Is this Father Sandoval here now?" I asked.

"Of course."

"We'll need to talk to him."

Parris looked at his watch. "It's quite late. Can't it wait?"

"No, it can't," Estelle said, her tone flat.

Parris turned from her to me, his eyes searching my face. "There's something you don't believe?"

I didn't see any point in sugarcoating it. "You lied to me once, Father. We have no way of knowing if you're lying now. If we talk with Father Sandoval and he confirms when he treated your ankle, that gives us something to go on."

"I'm telling you the truth."

"Perhaps. Is Sandoval here?"

Parris fell silent for a minute, then said as he stood up, "This is going to be a very public case after a while, isn't it?"

"What do you mean by that?"

"I mean it will all come out in the end…about Cecilia and me, about Daisy…all of it."

"I suppose it will," I said. I wasn't feeling kindly at the moment. It didn't bother me much that Parris might have to wallow for a while in his own mess. "I'll go with you to fetch Father Sandoval." Parris didn't argue.

We left Estelle in the front room and went upstairs. It was obvious that Parris's ankle really did hurt. Father Sandoval must have been waiting at his door because he answered Parris's light knock immediately.

Sandoval was the same priest who had greeted me on my first visit. He joined us downstairs and we made it brief. The older priest verified Parris's story, and my instincts told me that Father Mateo Sandoval was telling the absolute truth.

After Sandoval left the room, Parris looked relieved. Estelle snapped her notebook closed and stood up. "There's one more thing," she said. "Finn has no legitimate custody claim on Daisy."

"No, I suppose he doesn't," Parris said. I grimaced, because his tone said clearly to me, "I wish he did." Estelle read the same message on his face. She didn't raise her voice, but the words came out clipped and hard.

"Father Parris, I want Daisy out of the woods. And I want her out tomorrow."

The priest started to waffle. "I was going to talk with you about that," he said.

"I'm listening."

The man didn't know what to say. Maybe he couldn't

face H. T. Finn eye to eye…or maybe he was still unwilling to admit that his uncomplicated life at the retreat was over. I didn't know what the Catholic Church did to one of its priests who became a parent…and right then, that wasn't our concern.

"You're her father," Estelle said. "You can go up there with us tomorrow morning and take custody of the child. It's that simple. You are her father."

"I wish it were that simple," Parris said, and Estelle locked him with an icy glare.

"It *is* that simple," she said. "And between now and seven tomorrow morning when we pick you up, you might give some thought to the form your child support is going to take." She stood up and turned to me. "I have all I need."

As I stepped by him, I patted Parris on the shoulder. It was the sort of fatherly pat I might have given one of my sons after an ultimatum he didn't like. "Seven o'clock, Father," I said.

On the drive back home Estelle didn't say a word until we turned into the lane to the adobe. And then, so quietly I almost didn't hear, she said, "The fifth one."

"In the truck, you mean?"

She nodded. "If we find the fifth kid who was riding in that pickup truck, maybe we'll find the answers."

"Paul Garcia's been talking with Lucy Grider. Maybe he turned up something."

"I hope so. Otherwise, unless number five comes forward, we're going to have to sift through this community one person at a time."

"That won't be the first time we've done that." I glanced over at Estelle. She was chewing the corner of her lower lip, her forehead wrinkled in thought. I could have counted on one hand the number of times I'd heard Estelle express doubts when she'd been working on a case. She had an excuse this time. We hadn't enjoyed an extra minute to think things through or hunt for answers.

But this evening, as it turned out, the doubts weren't necessary. We didn't have to hunt. Kyle Osuna came to us.

he catches up with them, Waquie and Grider
gether. And maybe he finds out from the two of
who the others were."

aybe, maybe, maybe. Come on, Estelle. You saw
He couldn't care less."

could have happened that way."

'd have to be one fast worker, Estelle. In the first
we were up at his camp on Saturday, right after
ident with Cecilia Burgess."

may have found Waquie that morning…or later
fternoon."

would have had to. And then you're suggesting
the Lucero brothers and murders them. Nice
ut no evidence."

he's got Arajanian to help him."

. You don't have a scrap of evidence to sup-
"

ut there's possible motive," she said doggedly.
t's enough for a start." I was about to ques-
when we heard the thumping at the back door.
"You got a dog that wants in?"

don't." She got up and went into the kitchen.
d the curtain back a little and looked out.
s no outside light over that door, and she
ave seen a train if it had been parked on the
ulled the door open and I heard her suck in
n surprise.

e called and I sprang to my feet, dumping
per on the floor.

ed figure was sitting on the single wooden
ned sideways against the screen door, head
himpered a little, then lifted his head and
e."

# TWENTY

THE LIGHT WAS on over the front door at eleven that
night. The good doc was working late, called to the
clinic to set a broken arm. The arm belonged to one of
the Girl Scouts over at Camp Tracy, who'd done nothing more spectacular than fall off the top bunk during
a pillow fight.

Francis promised that he wouldn't take long—a
quick cast, a handful of aspirin, and the little girl would
be back in business. In a couple days she'd feel good
enough to use the heavy cast as a weapon and inflict
some real damage.

Estelle turned the light on after Francis left. I was
reading the Albuquerque afternoon paper and Estelle
was poring through her notes. She had talked for almost a half hour with Sheriff Tate on the telephone, and
Tate was just as frustrated as we were. He told Estelle
that all she had to do was say the word and she'd have
reinforcements, but she nixed the idea. In fact, leaving
men up on Quebrada Mesa was a waste of time. She
was sure that what had happened there was finished.
Tate didn't argue. If you put an army in the field, it
costs lots of bucks.

"All you can do is keep scratchin'," Tate had said.

"We're close," Estelle had told him. Close to what, I
wondered. The wave of murders was three-pronged…
Cecilia Burgess pitched out of the truck, Waquie and

Grider crushed in that same truck, with a neck snapped for good measure, and now the Lucero brothers.

Estelle was the only one who doubted that Cecil Lucero had pulled the trigger on his brother. I thought she was fishing and told her so. True, the entire scenario was based on assumptions. It was even an assumption—a grand one—that the Luceros had been in the truck with Waquie and Grider. Who the hell knew.

"You don't think Cecil Lucero is the key?" I asked, laying down the newspaper. Estelle shook her head. "You don't think he killed his brother?"

"No. It doesn't make sense, sir. The shots were fired from the lip of the arroyo, approximately twenty yards from where we found Kenneth Lucero's body. That's where Paul found the shell casings. Now why would Kenneth Lucero be walking or running up the arroyo bed?"

"He was being chased."

"By his brother? If his brother took him out there with the intention of killing him, what ruse did he use? That they would go hunting? If that was the case, why didn't Kenneth have a gun of his own?"

"Maybe he forced him out there."

"Come on, sir. Cecil would have had to make Kenneth drive and hold a rifle on him in the car. That's difficult to do. Why didn't Kenneth try to get away before they got out that far?" She stopped for breath. "You see? It's got so many holes..."

"Do you think the Luceros were involved in Waquie's and Grider's deaths then?"

"Maybe. I don't see someone who'd push a truck over a cliff, then snap a neck for good measure, using a rifle the next day."

"That's what we're missing," I s
tern to any of this. You think som
brothers. All right. Suppose tha
person was the one who killed th
was a creative son of a bitch...an
of a trail. If the incidents are un
less sense." As I saw it, our pr
like to work methodically, but
fire after another, without a m

Earlier in the evening, De
stopped by and summarized l
Grider. The girl had given hin
who might have been hanging
or the Lucero brothers that n
all had been together in the
names stood off the page fo

"Talk to each one of ther
overtime didn't bother eith
and Estelle had sent them

From out of the blue Est
all the information." I put d
staring into the open brief
the papers. "Parris told h
the truck. He even told Fi
Robert Waquie. How m
out who was involved?"

"Not much, I suppos
to be having problems."

"Just suppose Finn
"Just suppose. The pri
and Finn learns about
next day...we're wor
information. Finn fir

Wher
are to
them

"M
Finn.
"It
"He
place,
the acc
"He
in the a
"He
he finds
theory
"And
"Sure
port that
"No,
"And tha
tion that
I said,
"Sure
She pulle
There wa
couldn't h
step. She
breath wit
"Sir," sh
the newspa
A hunch
step. He lea
down. He w
said, "Pleas

My first thought had been that we'd collected a wandering drunk, but there was no inebriation in that voice…just hurt. "Now what the hell." I pushed past Estelle and tried to open the door, but he was blocking it. From the hunch of his shoulders and the hang of his head, he wasn't up to moving.

"Let me go around front," Estelle said, and she darted off, grabbing her flashlight from the kitchen counter. In seconds she appeared in the darkness. When the beam of the flashlight hit him in the face, the man cringed against the door. "No," he murmured.

"It's all right," Estelle said. "We're here." She saw the blood at the same time I did. A puddle was forming on the gray wood of the step.

"Move him away from the door so we can get him inside," I said. I slapped on the overhead kitchen light.

Estelle put her arm around the man's shoulders and tried to scrunch him sideways to the edge of the step. His head tipped back, and I saw that he was biting his lower lip so hard that he'd drawn blood.

With a grunt of agony he pushed himself to his feet, supported by Estelle on one side and stiff-arming the side of the house with his free hand. I held open the door, and the two of them careened into the kitchen. He dropped to his knees, taking Estelle with him, and then slumped over to curl on the floor in a fetal position. "The door," he whispered. "Close the door." I did so. Now that he was in the light, I could see that he wasn't more than a kid, maybe twenty at the most. And he was wearing the universal kid's summer uniform—running shoes, faded blue jeans, and T-shirt. And if he bled much more, he wouldn't live to be older than a kid. His left side was soaked with blood from lower ribs to knee. And what wasn't bloody was dripping wet, caked here and there with fresh mud.

I knelt down. "You hold the flashlight," I said. The overhead light fixture held one of those useless sixty-watt bulbs that threw just enough light so you didn't bark your shins on the table and chairs.

The kid lay with his head on the cool linoleum, eyes closed, breath rapid and shallow. I pulled up the blood-soaked T-shirt. "Jesus Christ," I said. "Hold the light over here." I pried his right hand loose from where it was clamped to his side.

He was leaking from two places. The entry wound was a pencil-sized, punched hole a hand's width from his spine, right on the second floating rib from the bottom.

The projectile had blown right through him, exiting by taking out the front end of the same rib. The exit wound wasn't neat and was as big as a quarter. It bled copiously, and I guessed the bullet had nicked either the kid's stomach or kidney or both. I yanked a dish towel off the side rack by the sink and made a large pad.

"Make sure Francis is still at the clinic," I said, but Estelle was already moving. "Can you hold that in place?" I asked, and the kid nodded slightly. His hand drifted back and rested on the towel. "I'll be right back," I added. He wasn't going anywhere, but the last thing someone wants who's hurt badly is to go solo.

On the way out through the living room, I jerked the old army blanket off the sofa. It only took a minute to arrange the back of the Blazer so he'd have a place to lie, and by the time I trotted back into the house, Estelle was back in the kitchen, kneeling by the kid. She looked up and said, "He's there."

"There's no time to wait for an ambulance. We'll take mine. There's some room in the back." Estelle helped me pick him up and I carried him out to the Blazer, ducking sideways so I didn't whack his skull on the doorjambs. It was a good thing for him and me both that he was slightly built.

Estelle rode in the back with him, keeping the pressure on the dressing. In less than three minutes we were swinging into the parking lot of the clinic. I saw Mary Vallo's old pickup truck and murmured thanks. I wasn't much of a nurse.

Francis Guzman was organized and waiting. He had already called the ambulance for a transfer to Albuquerque. He and Mary Vallo worked quickly to stabilize the kid. Before I had time to catch my breath, he was stuck with needles in both arms, with chemicals going in from one side and whole blood from the other.

Guzman debrided the exit wound enough so that he could see what was what.

At one point he said, "Well, that's good," and continued working. I leaned against the wall and watched. Mary Vallo was damned close to a mind reader. Only once or twice did Francis Guzman have to verbalize what he needed.

"Sir?"

I turned and looked down the hall. Estelle had the contents of the kid's wallet spread on the coffee table in the waiting room. It wasn't much of a display.

I walked out and sat down beside her. "Who is he?"

She held up the driver's license. "Kyle Osuna. San Estevan. He's nineteen."

"I wonder who the hell he crossed," I said.

Estelle tossed the license down. It fell on three one-dollar bills. The license and the money were it.

"Estelle?" Francis beckoned his wife, and I followed her back into the examining room. The young doctor spoke with confidence. "The ambulance will be here any minute and we'll want to transport. But he's conscious and lucid so you might take your best shot now. He'll go into surgery, and it'll be tomorrow morning before you can talk with him again."

"How is he doing, Francis?" I asked.

Guzman put his hands on his hips and regarded the still form on the table. One of the kid's hands twitched, and Mary Vallo rested her hand on his forearm. "He'll be fine. It's not as bad as it probably looked when he was bleeding all over the kitchen floor." He flashed a grin at me as if this sort of thing happened all the time. "What's the story?"

"I don't know," I said. "That's what Whiz Kid needs to find out." Estelle stood beside Osuna's shoulder with Mary Vallo on the other side. Two faces like those would have been enough to convince any patient that he'd died and gone to heaven. I stood at the foot of the bed and took notes in shorthand.

"Can you tell me your name?" Estelle asked.

"Kyle Osuna." The kid's eyes focused on Estelle's face.

"Kyle, do you know who shot you?"

"No." He took a shallow breath.

"Did you see the person who shot you?"

"Yes." He frowned, probably trying to think straight as the intravenous Valium fogged more than the pain.

"Can you describe him for me?"

"He was…he had long white hair."

"White hair? He was an old man?"

"No." Kyle closed his eyes, and his right hand lifted and started to drift over toward the dressing covering the wound. Mary intercepted and held his hand in hers, careful that she didn't dislodge the I.V. "He was young."

"Do you mean blond hair? Very light?" I heard the crunch of tires pulling into the clinic's driveway, and Francis went out to meet the ambulance crew.

"Yes," Kyle Osuna said. "Very light." He took a deep breath, very slowly. "He's about my age. Thin, not too tall. About my size. I've seen him around some."

"But you don't know his name?"

"No."

"Do you know where he lives? Does he live around here?" Osuna nodded slightly.

"I've seen him a few times. I don't know where he lives."

"Can you tell me what happened? Why he shot you?"

"I was walking up the highway from my house. I was going to come talk to you. He was walking the other way, just about by the trading post. He knew my name. He asked if I had a cigarette. I said no and kept walking. That's when…" He paused and looked over at me. "That's when I heard this noise. Like a metal latch or something. I turned and saw that he was just standing on the shoulder of the road. And right away I saw that he had a gun of some kind. I freaked, man. So I ran."

"You could see the gun in the dark?"

"There's that light by the trading post parking lot."

"And he chased you?"

"No. He shot me. I didn't hear the gun. But it

knocked me down. At first I thought maybe he'd chased me and hit me with his fist. But then I looked back and he was still standing there. He hadn't moved none. Just standing there. And then he started to walk up the road toward me. Real slow."

The ambulance attendants brought the gurney down the hall into the examining room. If we wanted to know more, we'd have to ride the ambulance to Albuquerque.

"What happened then?" Estelle persisted.

"I got up and ran into the orchard there and made it over toward the river. That's when it started to hurt. It hurt so bad and I was scared. I thought that maybe with all the brush he couldn't follow me. There's a hundred places to hide. After a few minutes I thought I heard him running up the highway. I'm not sure."

The attendants moved into position and Estelle held up a hand, gaining a few seconds.

"Do you know why he shot you, Kyle?"

"Yes."

"Why?"

"Because I was in the truck when the girl was killed, just like them." He closed his eyes tightly and bit his already bloody lip. "That's why I was coming to see you. The other four, they got murdered. I heard about Kenny and Cecil...I got so scared."

Estelle's eyes locked on mine, and I could see the triumph on her face. "Arajanian," she said and headed for the door. I should have shared her excitement, but it was dread that twisted my gut. I knew Estelle, and I already knew exactly what mistake she was going to make.

# TWENTY-ONE

ESTELLE REYES-GUZMAN'S first move couldn't have been more logical. If Kyle Osuna survived, and Dr. Guzman assured us that he would, then he would be charged either with the murder of Cecilia Burgess or as an accessory to murder, depending on how his story developed. Either felony would go a long way toward making Osuna's convalescence painful.

Estelle used the telephone in the clinic to call her county dispatch and made sure that two deputies would meet the ambulance when it arrived in Albuquerque.

We'd been caught unaware, but Tate wouldn't be. In Albuquerque, the deputies would have a file photo of Arajanian. If Osuna was lucid before he went to surgery, they'd make sure he saw the photograph. *If.* I knew the odds of that were small, with his system battered by shock and painkillers.

Estelle wasn't willing to wait. Her mind was made up, set in concrete.

By the time we pulled into the driveway of the house, I was ready to yell at her as if she were a wayward teenager.

I parked the Blazer and she sat in the passenger seat, making no move toward the door handle.

"In the first place," she said, "no judge is going to give me an arrest warrant for Robert Arajanian unless Osuna I.D.'s him from a photo. Not on the evidence we have." She ticked off on her fingers the meager points. "One, we suspect him. Two, Kyle Osuna says his assailant had blond hair and was skinny. That could be Arajanian, or it could just as easily be someone else."

"Yeah, there are dozens of blondies in this valley," I said with heavy sarcasm. "Whole tribes of 'em."

She ignored that and plunged on. "We know Arajanian has a gun but not what kind. And we don't know what caliber weapon was used to shoot Osuna."

"It wasn't a .22."

"No, it obviously wasn't." She opened the door of the Blazer and stepped out. "The only way we're going to get anywhere is to go up there and confront Arajanian. And Finn. You can bet that he's behind it...that Arajanian does just what Finn tells him to." I slammed the steering wheel with the base of my hand. "Damn it, Estelle. What's wrong with you? If we left right now, it'd be two in the morning before we could get there."

"That's what I mean. The darkness would be to our advantage. They'd never expect it."

"For Christ's sake," I muttered and got out. I followed her into the house. "Think a little. Think about this: If Finn and Arajanian are guilty—and I say *if*— look at their track record. They managed to lure two healthy young toughs over the edge of Quebrada Mesa. We don't know how the hell they did that, but it's a fact. And then, cool as a snake, one or both break Grider's neck. That's cold-blooded and they did it under cover of darkness."

Estelle raised an eyebrow as if to say, "So what?"

"And then, if they're the guilty parties, they somehow managed to bushwhack the Lucero brothers...and neither one of those boys looked like your basic wimp.

We don't know when that happened, but it wouldn't surprise me if it happened at night. And notice that seven shots were placed in a saucer-sized target at more than twenty yards…so fast that the victim didn't have time to twist and vary the wound paths.

"And then, finally," I held up a hand to stave off her rejoinder, "if he's guilty, like you're sure he is, Arajanian shot Kyle Osuna in the middle of San Estevan… at night, with a silencer-equipped handgun. Hit him pretty solidly, too. But no one can bat a thousand all the time. So the killer screws up just a tad. The bullet is an inch too low and wide. He doesn't get a chance for another because Kyle Osuna is spooked into being jackrabbit-fast on his feet."

"If we wait until dawn," Estelle said with great patience, "then both you and I know that they'll be gone. And Daisy will be gone right along with them."

"We don't know that. And I share your concern for the kid. But you're letting your emotions rule. There's nothing to be gained by rushing in half-cocked."

"Sir," she said as if I'd added two and two and gotten five. All the time I had been talking, Estelle had been buttoning on her bullet-proof vest.

"Arajanian knows the boy got away," she said. "Now maybe he's stupid enough to think Kyle Osuna crawled off into the bushes and died, but I don't think so. It's logical to assume that someone who is fit enough to jump up after being knocked flat by a bullet can maybe make it to help. It's a good chance. Would you just sit up there in the woods, waiting for us to come and arrest you?"

"I might. If I knew there was no direct evidence against me, I might think that it was better to wait and keep my eyes and ears open for movement of the troops."

"And all this time Daisy is up there. You know who she's with, don't you? She's with two freaks who have managed to kill five people. I'm not about to wait a minute longer than I have to. If I'm wrong, then I'll be the first to apologize to Finn and Arajanian, face-to-face."

"No, Estelle. If you're wrong, you'll probably get us both killed. And maybe Daisy, too." I snapped my lighter, touched the flame to the cigarette, and promptly coughed so hard my eyes swam with tears.

Estelle waited until the spasm passed before saying, "I'm not asking you to go up there with me, sir."

"I'm charmed," I managed to say, and when I caught my breath I held up a hand. "Will you at least grant me a condition or two?"

That stubborn eyebrow went up, saying, "Let me hear it first."

"First, let's be a little smart and have some backup. Call Garcia and Martinez. Leave Martinez with the vehicles in the campground so we've got radio communication with dispatch if we need it. We can reach Martinez with the hand-held."

Estelle nodded. "And?"

"Listen to an old marine, Estelle. If Finn and Arajanian have done what we think they have, we're going against two cold hands. Unless we can take them completely by surprise, it won't work. Remember that ridge that runs along the creek, up above the campsite on the west side?"

"Sure."

"All right. If we follow that instead of the creek bed,

we'll have some protection and the opportunity to see the camp before we approach it. We're going to want to make damn sure that we know what's what before we go in there."

Estelle frowned. "That's all?"

"All?" I said. "No.... Most important, we aren't going there at all until dawn, with about thirty-five state police and deputies behind us...and maybe a helicopter or two."

"The more people are involved, the more chance there is for Daisy to get hurt. Remember when we busted the gold diggers down in Posadas?"

I remembered that well. We'd been part of a grand night-time embarrassment that included, among other things, a customs agent holding a cocked magnum on his spread-eagled prisoner...and then finding out when someone swung a flashlight around that he was guarding nothing but an empty down jacket, crumpled around the base of a cactus. Everybody had been so nervous that if a trigger had been pulled, twenty lawmen would have been plugged by their own compadres.

"We can slip in and out and use the darkness as a cover," Estelle said. "It's safer at night with just a few of us." She added, "I've got another vest at the office you can use."

I stared at her in disbelief. "I suppose the other alternative is to handcuff you to the bedpost," I said, and Estelle gave me that fetching smile that lighted her face.

"You could try, sir." She could melt ice at absolute zero.

"You and your unborn child...who by the way has nothing to gain from any of this." As I said that, Estelle's smile faded and she regarded me evenly.

"I'm not helpless, sir."

"I know you're not. And sometimes I wish you god-damn were, that's all."

That earned me a fleeting grin, but she was determined. I could call Pat Tate and have him try to order some sense into her head, but her car would be kicking dust before the call was completed.

I took a deep breath. "That vest had better be size triple X," I said. Hell, I couldn't let her go alone. Paul Garcia was a rookie. Martinez had a wife, two kids, and another baby on the way, so he'd stay with the car...at least I could make damn sure of that.

We walked out to the patrol car. I made sure that the plastic ammo wallet I carried in my hip pocket had all eighteen rounds and that the magnum held its six. I got in, muttering all the while.

"What did you say, sir?"

"I said I don't even work for this county. This is ridiculous."

"Yes, sir." Estelle backed out of the driveway and I tried one last card.

"If Francis hadn't gone to Albuquerque with the ambulance, would he have let you do this?"

"Probably not, sir."

"But you would have done it anyway."

"Yes, sir." Her jaw had that stubborn, resolute set. I knew that she intended to rescue little Daisy, just like in the fairy tales. I didn't like the only ending I could imagine.

# TWENTY-TWO

THE MOON WAS huge and bright. It shone into Steamboat Rock Canyon like a gigantic spotlight. When I stepped out of Estelle's patrol car in the campground parking lot, I could see my shadow. Garcia and Martinez waited.

The moon-washed air was dead. I hitched my gun a little higher under the overhang of my gut. Not a stir through the pine needles, not a whisper down the halls of the canyon. Nothing. I sighed.

"They better be sound sleepers," I muttered and watched Paul Garcia thumb five fat cartridges into his shotgun. He was nervous and that would keep him alert. Martinez fidgeted. He didn't much like staying behind.

Except for the three vehicles and Al Martinez, the campground was deserted as we started up the trail through the silent forest. We reached the fork of the trail, and then we veered even farther to the north, cutting away from the trail and following the granite spine of the ridge that paralleled the creek. I tried to breathe quietly, but after a few yards I was rasping like an old steam engine. Estelle slowed some, and when we reached a rock outcropping fifty yards above the trail fork she stopped.

I sat down on one of the ledges with a grunt. My

pulse slammed in my ears, and out of habit I counted it for a minute.

"This is crazy," I whispered.

"We'll take it easy," Estelle murmured.

"It's still crazy." I took a deep breath. The banging in my ears receded a little. The smells were rich, floating up from where our boots crushed the pine needles, grasses, and herbs. "When we reach the top of this ridge, it's going to be rough. If one of us kicks a single pebble, the sound's going to carry."

Estelle nodded and repeated herself. "We'll take it easy."

I stood up and looked ahead. "I'm ready." We faced perhaps a hundred yards of open rock slide and then the timber capped the granite ridge.

One rock at a time was my pace. I made sure of my footing before trusting my weight to wobbly ankles.

I reached the trees, and both Estelle and Paul made motions as if they were ready to move on. I held up a hand. Tour guides were all alike. They rushed ahead to the next attraction and waited for the old tourists who were poking along behind. When everyone caught up, it was time to be off again. The guys bringing up the rear, gasping because of bad hearts or recent hernias, never got to stop and rest. "We should have called for a helicopter," I said.

"Are you all right?" Estelle asked, and I waved a hand.

"Just fine. I love hiking, don't you? Especially in the middle of the goddamn night when I can't see where to put my goddamn feet." I turned and surveyed the hillside. The terrain swept up steadily, curving off slightly toward the east.

Estelle whispered, "If we just stay on the highest line, we should be just right."

"Let me lead," I said. I was under no illusions that I was the most competent woodsman of the group or even that I had the best nose for direction. But I hated being there more than the other two did, and because of that I might make fewer mistakes.

Hell, Estelle had time to take up knitting lessons while she waited for me to select steps. But we made progress. I passed a big, mistletoe-twisted ponderosa and saw rocks jutting out to the right toward the canyon.

I turned and held a finger over my lips. Both Estelle and Paul stopped. I made my way in slow motion out on the outcropping. I could see, off to the south, where the two canyons joined down by the creek. If my distance judgment was correct, the hot springs were less than a quarter mile away.

I remembered…it seemed a year now rather than a day…seeing Finn and little Daisy walk down through the timber. The slope hadn't been extreme. That was the route we should take, coming in from the north behind the tent site.

I grunted up from my squatting position and waved for Estelle and Paul to follow. As we drew away from the terminus of the ridge and worked toward its root where it joined the mesa top, the pines were widely spaced, a park stand that would have been lovely to a Forest Service timber cruiser.

The ridge's spine curved to the right, and I knew it circled behind the campsites below. I stopped. Estelle stepped so close I could smell the faint aroma of the shampoo she'd used.

"We'll come in right behind them," I whispered. She nodded. I motioned to Paul Garcia and laid a hand on his shoulder. "We don't want to go down the hill as a group. Spread out and watch your footing. You on the left, Paul, with Estelle over on the right. Don't get ahead of me. Don't rush."

His head bobbed with excitement, but I didn't release my grip on his shoulder. "When we're about a hundred feet from the camp, I want to stop and listen. You watch for my signal. And we'll stay there for a while, so don't get in a hurry."

The footing was easy. I kept the inchworm pace, giving each boot toe plenty of time to find twigs or sticks that waited to let out rifle-shot cracks. Like three ghosts, we moved down through the timber.

The moonlight was broken into soft patches by the forest canopy, but before long I could make out Finn's tent. The black rectangle was a geometry out of place in the tapestry of irregular shapes.

I held up a hand and stopped. To my right, I could see Estelle.

She stood at the base of a ponderosa that was thick enough to hide three of her. With the authority of her uniform stripped away by the night, her figure was almost that of a child. The outline of her Stetson reminded me of the flat brim of an Easter bonnet worn by a girl a century ago.

I twisted at the waist and for a moment Paul Garcia remained invisible. Almost all the images in the nighttime forest were vertical…everything else disappeared.

My eyes clicked from tree to tree until I found him. He was leaning against a pine as if he were taking a breather during a Sunday afternoon stroll. He must have taken off his Stetson, because I could see the curved outline of the top of his head.

He pushed away from the tree and took a half step forward. I stopped breathing as I saw the moonlight touch the blond hair that swept down to his shoulders.

# TWENTY-THREE

When I realized the ghost off to my left was Robert Arajanian and not Deputy Paul Garcia, I took an involuntary step forward.

The object in his right hand wasn't a flashlight. He held the heavy automatic pistol with its muzzle pointing up. I could see the bulbous silencer.

Maybe Arajanian had deliberately chosen the young deputy as his first target. Garcia was carrying the shotgun and would appear to pose the most obvious threat. Maybe Arajanian had been padding along behind us, just keeping tabs. I had my answer soon enough.

When he knew I'd seen him, Arajanian twisted at the waist. The silenced automatic pistol swung toward me. I didn't have time to shout at him or plead or reason.

Arajanian's mistake was shooting at me. I was the least threat. I'd been on the planet long enough to be cautious…and that was coupled with reactions and physical abilities far from athletic. But my instincts were honed, even if the old body didn't provide much backup.

The blond-haired killer wasn't there to talk. I knew Arajanian was going to shoot before he pulled the trigger, and I threw myself sideways toward the nearest ponderosa. The bullet gouged pine and spat bark in my face.

The automatic didn't make much noise…just a nasty little sneeze with some clattering as the slide jarred backward to fling out the empty case and ram another cartridge into the chamber.

But in the silence of the pines Robert Arajanian might as well have fired a howitzer.

Deputy Paul Garcia's nerves were wired. He was less than six months out of the academy, where instructors teach the rookies all the right moves. He was young and athletic.

Robert Arajanian wasn't allowed a second mistake. Garcia crouched and pivoted in one fluid motion. One knee hit the ground as support even as the twelve-gauge came up. He had enough moonlight and a clear target. Arajanian's arm was outstretched, the big automatic and its silencer flashing moonbeams. I scrambled for cover.

I heard the shotgun's pump action only as an extension of the explosion. The muzzle flash of the big gun lit up the hillside. Instinctively I ducked my head. Off to the left I heard a thump as Arajanian's pistol flew out of his hand, and then an awful gurgling and choking.

"Christ, no!" I gasped. My intake of breath was so violent I sucked pine duff and choked. I spat and panted for breath, at the same time trying to draw my own magnum. I lay motionless. Arajanian might not be alone, and I didn't know which way to turn. To make matters worse, I knew Garcia's finger was still tense on the trigger of the shotgun.

I moved my head a fraction. I could see only Arajanian's legs from the knees down.

"Paul," I said, keeping my voice low and even, "hold

your fire. Nobody move." I pulled myself up beside the pine trunk. Garcia was crouched thirty feet downhill.

Beyond, the tent was dark and quiet. Where the hell was Finn? I cursed eloquently. What a goddamn mess. Any hope of surprise was gone. But maybe the camp was empty. The hairs stood up on the back of my neck, and I ducked and looked uphill, scanning the hillside. Nothing.

"Paul, are you all right?" I said quietly.

"Yes, sir."

"Estelle, stay put," I said, a little louder. I glanced over my shoulder at the spot where I'd last seen her. She hadn't moved, but I could see moonlight glint on her service revolver. "Paul," I said, "hold position."

"Yes, sir." There was a little tremor in his voice, but he wasn't going to do anything stupid.

I pulled the small flashlight out of my coat pocket. With the revolver in my right hand and the light held well away from my body with the other, I crouched and stepped toward Robert Arajanian.

My light caught the glint of the automatic, and I detoured cautiously to pick it up, then shove it into my belt. It was a heavy frame Beretta...no kid's gun.

Arajanian lay on his back. His heart was still beating, but he'd stopped struggling and he'd stopped breathing.

The blast of double zero buckshot had hit him a terrible, slashing blow at the base of the throat. Even as I knelt with the light I saw the pulse subside in the torn left carotid artery. His left hand lifted, opened wide, and then slowly drifted down to rest lightly on his blood-soaked chest. His eyes stared up into the night.

The kid wasn't going to give us any answers. That

left H. T. Finn. I straightened up. There was still no sign of life in the tent. Would the son of a bitch just let us walk into camp? Was he waiting in the musty darkness of the tent, weapon ready, with one hand clamped over Daisy's mouth to stifle whimpers? Or was he waiting for us, hidden behind a black tree trunk, invisible and deadly?

I whispered a withering curse at my own overactive imagination. In all likelihood, Finn was long gone with Daisy pulled along for the ride.

I took a deep breath. I blinked the light at Estelle quickly, then held it so that it illuminated my own right hand. I beckoned her over, then turned the light off. I moved off to the side a little and waited.

Garcia hesitated, then crept slowly up the hill. He wasn't in a hurry to see what he'd done. When he was within whispering distance, I reached out and touched his shoulder.

"You did the right thing," I said. He stared down at Arajanian, then looked away. I could hear Estelle's quick breathing.

"Is he dead?" she asked.

"Yes. It's Arajanian."

"Was he going to shoot?"

"He did shoot," I whispered. "Once at me. That's all he had time for."

She looked downhill at the dark blob of the tent.

"I want you two to stay up here for a minute," I said. "Arajanian knew we were coming…there's no way of telling how long he was on our heels. Maybe all the way from the parking lot. But if he knew, then that means Finn does, too."

Estelle shook her head. "Listen," she said and her

whisper was almost harsh. I couldn't see her face under
the brim of the Stetson, but I knew her black eyes were
drilling mine. "If he's down there, then there's a better
chance with the three of us. We stay spread out, just
the way we were."

Garcia's whisper was filled with tension. "And the
more Finn knows that he doesn't have a chance, the
better the odds are that he'll give it up."

I might have agreed with the deputy almost any
other time. But Finn was no panic-stricken teenager
cornered in an alley after hitting a convenience store.
That sort of mentality I could understand. But Finn?
He was an unknown.

I thought of another chilling possibility. "Maybe
Arajanian killed Finn," I said.

"No," Estelle said. "Arajanian did as he was told. I
could see that. And nothing else makes sense."

I hesitated. I wanted a plan without risk. There
wasn't one, except to wait until dawn and ring the place
with troops. And then the only person who'd suffer
would be Daisy…if she hadn't suffered already. "We're
wasting time," I muttered.

Estelle motioned Paul Garcia into position. In the
moonlight I could see that his face was as pale as Arajanian's. His forehead was shiny with sweat, but he
clutched the shotgun at high port, trigger finger out
of the guard. He'd be all right. We turned and started
down through the trees.

The three of us were spooked…but probably still
thinking we could control events if we were careful
enough. We reached the bottom of the slope where it
splayed out into the narrow swale. I held up my hand

and we stopped. The tent was twenty feet in front of me, the entry flaps on the opposite side, facing downhill.

I listened, my head cocked slightly. Nothing. No wisp of smoke rose from the ashes in the stone fire circle. A slight breeze was stirring the tops of the ponderosas, a signal that dawn wasn't many hours away. I turned and caught Paul Garcia's eye. I pointed to a spot between me and the tent. He nodded. I moved slowly to the side, toward Estelle. I wanted her off to the side of the door flaps. If I angled in from the other side, that would give us the best coverage.

With infinite care and listening so hard my ears hurt, I circled the tent until I was looking directly at the front flap. Again, I stopped. The silence was so deep that the normal ringing of my ears was a scream of head-noise.

I narrowed my eyes as if that would help me see through the tightly woven nylon. Just about the time when I had decided the place was deserted, I heard the noise. It wasn't a cry, nor a whimper. Just the faintest sniffle, like a person would make when his nose is tickling. Estelle heard it, too, because she immediately took a step toward the tent.

I held up my hand sharply, and she stopped. We waited, and after a minute Estelle shifted position restlessly. As if that motion were a signal, we heard the noise again. Someone was in the tent. And whoever it was hadn't been as patient as we were.

Estelle Reyes made her decision before I had a chance to move. She took three quick steps to the tent. She held her flashlight to one side and jerked the tent flap, hard. A frightened whimper greeted her. And this time I recognized the voice as a child's.

"It's Daisy," Estelle said, turning toward me so that I would hear. I took a step forward. The first rifle shot came from behind me, so loud that it numbed like a dynamite blast. Paul Garcia's shotgun pinwheeled through the air, hit the side of the tent, and bounced to the ground. If the deputy made a sound, I didn't hear it. He disappeared behind the tent.

"Get down!" I shouted. Estelle was crouched in the doorway of the tent with nowhere to go. I was out in the open, without a target. I thumbed the hammer of my revolver back, turned, and saw motion downstream by the boulders. I snapped off a single shot and then tried to sprint off to the right to draw fire away from Estelle and the child.

My right ankle collapsed, and I staggered sideways, fighting for balance. The rifle blasted again, and this time I saw the flash out of the corner of my eye. Something tugged hard at the back of my vest. I fell awkwardly and lost my grip on the revolver. Three rapid shots cracked out from my left, and I heard one of the slugs from Estelle's revolver ricochet off the boulder and whine into the timber like a demented insect.

I was looking at the rock when the rifle fired, and I saw the massive corona of muzzle blast. The front corner of the tent collapsed, and it took an awful eternity for me to realize that it had been Estelle Reyes's body spinning into the rope and support rods that brought the tent down.

## TWENTY-FOUR

I SCREAMED SOMETHING—I don't remember what, then lunged for my revolver, snapped it up, and yanked the trigger. I fired twice, so blinded by the muzzle flash from the two-inch barrel that I lost the target.

I tried to stand, lost my balance, and fell to my hands and knees, the revolver digging into the dirt. I heard the scuffle of feet on pebbles. I straightened up and held the revolver in both hands. I saw the ghost of motion and fired twice. The rifle crashed out again, and this time the blast corona was perfectly symmetrical, with me in the focus.

The rifle bullet jerked me backward. The revolver flew off into the night. I landed hard on my back and felt an agonizing stab of pain as the automatic pistol I'd picked up and shoved into my belt dug into my spine.

I heard scuffling in the rocks down by the first of the springs. I tried to inch my right hand around to the automatic, but that arm wouldn't work. Someone cleared his throat and I froze, waiting.

His feet on the pine duff didn't make much noise. A circle of light poured over me.

I heard a "tsk," like a man sucking on a toothpick as he surveys the remains of a big feast.

"Ah, you people," H. T. Finn said passively. He "tsked" again.

The light moved out of my eyes, and I could

out the rifle that he now rested on his shoulder as a deer hunter might. Both my hands were in sight and they both were empty.

He bent down and picked up my handgun, then flung it so hard I heard it clatter on rocks on the other side of the swale. "Such a waste, isn't it?" he murmured and then moved off. I was able to twist my head a fraction and grimaced against the pain. He walked to the tent. He looked down at Estelle Reyes for a brief moment, then nudged her out of the way. He bent down, picked up something, and threw it off into the darkness.

"Ruth?" he called softly. "Ruth, it's all right. You're safe now." He knelt at the door of the tent, holding up the sagging nylon and broken support rod. The little girl emerged. It was too dark to see her face. She wrapped her arms around Finn's neck. He stood up, lifting the girl effortlessly. "That's my girl," he said. "So brave." He ran a hand through her hair. "So brave."

She whispered something and Finn said, "I know. I know. But let's finish here." He moved away from the tent and bent to let Daisy stand on her own. He took her by the hand and they walked down the swale toward the boulders. He said something else to her that my fuzzed brain didn't understand and then returned alone.

I managed to find my right arm…it felt detached and jointless…and pulled it across my stomach for support. I rolled to my left side. Finn stood quietly for a minute, watching me. "Perhaps a little struggle will be good for your soul," he said, hefting the rifle.

"You son of a bitch," I mumbled, but he wasn't interested in conversation. And maybe when it came to face-to-face bloodletting he couldn't stomach being as efficient as Anglian.

He walked
darting far ah
the kid's c
that on
was lo
of
o

osed so tightly
wrinkles.
loser. Her
od, and i
r. I sw
n my
be
rchase,
ingers found the poo
d made a mess of folding it agai
d position again and crunched my
le's flashlight. I breathed a sigh of
ndkerchief, and grabbed the light.
de it impossible to see her scalp,
ertain light. But it appeared that
r the crown of her head on the
d's spread behind and above the
way of knowing what damage
ne, but she was breathing and

tucked the light in my armpit.
ief was a lousy bandage, but
e bleeding. I gently pressed it
groaned faintly.
I whispered. "You can do it."
himpering noise, and one of
up toward her skull.
ace?" I asked as her hand
ice was soft enough that it
e her already busted skull.
I felt her fingers close on

said urgently. I eased her

ground shut, cl
with a thousand

I hunkered c
heavy with bloo
ground under he
kerchief. It was i
ward and reached

Using that as pu
my waist until my f
the handkerchief ar
my thigh. I change
knee down on Estel
relief, dropped the ha

Her thick hair ma
especially in the unc
the bullet had hit nea
right side, nearly a han
tip of her ear. I had no
the rifle bullet had do
had a strong pulse.

I curled my arm and
The wadded handkerch
it might stop some of th
against her skull. Estelle

"Come on, hard head,"
Estelle made a small w
her hands started to crab

"Can you hold it in pl
found mine. I hoped r v
wouldn't crash around ir si

"Eh," she whispered, a n
the cotton.

"I've got to help Paul," I

head down, leaned back, and, using the flashlight as
a short cane, pried myself to my feet. I swayed like a
drunk, but my ankle was too numb to care. I turned
carefully, playing the light past the tent. Paul Garcia
hadn't moved.

There was nothing that I or anyone else could do
for the deputy. The rifle bullet had struck Paul Garcia
high on the left cheek, just under his eye. Most of the
back of his skull was missing.

I straightened up, sick at heart. The radio. A small
part of my brain that was still working remembered
the hand-held radio. I staggered back to Estelle and
saw that the radio holster on her belt was empty—the
hand-held was what Finn had tossed so negligently off
into the trees.

"Run," I thought aloud, trying to will my words
downhill and into Deputy Al Martinez's mind. "Run
the other way." But he wouldn't do that. He would
have heard the shots. Maybe he would have radioed for
backup —radioed to a dispatcher seventy miles away.
But he wouldn't wait. He'd immediately charge up the
trail, right into Finn's gun. I swore, feeling helpless,
checkmated.

I desperately wanted that radio and swung the light
this way and that, trying to remember how Finn had
been standing when he pulled it out of Estelle's belt
holster. It was impossible. I saw Estelle's magnum and
made my way over to it. By collapsing back down to
my knees, I could pick it up. What the hell good it was
I didn't know.

It would take us a week to crawl down to the parking lot—by the time help arrived from Albuquerque,
the vultures would have us. Maybe Al Martinez would

play it smart. Like hell he would. I swore again—about all the expertise I could offer.

And then I sucked in my breath as another sound caught my attention. Behind me the pine forest was alive with a symphony of cracks, snaps, and a background beat that was a pulsing, loud, ominous roar. I turned and saw the light through the trees and at the same time felt the air fleeing uphill, nudging my cheeks. I don't know why I was surprised. Maybe I'd been hoping H. T. Finn would change his mind. Maybe I'd been hoping he was a human being. But he hadn't changed his mind. He'd probably even talked little Daisy into lending a hand.

The Smokey Bear signs along the highway warned about a careless match or cigarette. Smokey hadn't met H. T. Finn. The bastard had used two gallons of white gasoline to set the mountain on fire.

# TWENTY-FIVE

THE FIRE HUGGED the ground, bright enough to highlight the smoke clouds. The blaze generated its own breeze, which mixed with the morning updraft in the swale. Neither Estelle nor I could run up the mountain ahead of it.

Garcia's shotgun lay beside the back of the tent, and I grabbed it to use as a crutch. Estelle hadn't changed position, and her face was still frozen in that awful grimace.

"You have to help me, babe," I said, resting my left hand on her forehead. One eyelid flickered a little, and she nodded slightly. "Can you understand me?"

Again she nodded just enough that I felt the motion of her head in my hand.

"I can't carry you unless you can sit up some." This time she opened her left eye just a crack. It was a terrible imitation of one of her favorite expressions of doubt, that wonderful raised eyebrow that I'd earned a thousand times over the years.

"We have to make it to the pool down by the spring," I said. "The son of a bitch set the woods on fire." I put my hand under her, at the base of her neck, trying to support both her head and shoulders with one hand. She pushed against the ground with both hands. Her teeth ground together with the effort. A sigh of pain escaped as she leaned on my shoulder. I paused to regain my breath. She was now sitting, her feet straight out in front of her. I was kneeling beside her, my arm around her shoulders.

"Do you think you can walk?" I asked.

"Uh," she said.

The fire was now so loud that I had to shout. "Can you stand?"

"Uh-uh."

"Shit," I said. I looked over my shoulder, hoping to see a couple of ambulance attendants with a gurney. All I saw were bright flames, arching high into the sky, reaching to the very tops of the ponderosa pines. Smoke rolled in rich, thundering billows, obscuring the stars and moon. We didn't have to worry about light. The fire would give us plenty—until it roasted us.

I could have easily picked her up if I'd had two good arms. If she weighed more than a hundred pounds, it was only because of the cop junk strapped to her waist and the bullet-proof vest that hadn't done her head a bit of good.

"Hold on to my neck," I said loudly. There was no immediate response. She'd drifted off into some other, less painful world.

I rolled Estelle onto her stomach. With the shotgun crutch jammed under my ruined right arm, I bent down just enough to grab the center of her Sam Browne belt.

If nothing else, my arms had gained some strength over the years with the constant exercise of pushing my own bulk up and out of chairs. I hauled Estelle up at the waist, the way an angry father might grab the belt of a three-year-old who'd been dashing for cover. She felt like a sack of grain, folded in the middle.

There wasn't time to worry about prenatal care. If

her pregnancy survived this night, the kid would be one tough hombre.

The effort brought her back to consciousness. She tried to balance, then fell backward against me. I knelt on my right knee, her weight resting on my left leg. I released her belt and flung my arm around her before she had a chance to fall on her face, then hugged her close.

"Now we're both going to stand up," I said after I caught my breath. Her left hand came up and held the top of her head. She turned slightly so that she could curl the other arm around my neck. My handkerchief was still glued to her skull. We both stood up, shaky and gasping. Any other time we would have collapsed with laughter.

Like two drunks tied together in a three-legged race, we lurched down the swale toward the fire. The wind was picking up as the fire generated its own vortices.

We passed the boulder that had been the gateway to the campsite. The first spring, high in the rocks to the right, dribbled a trickle of sweet sulfur water down into a puddle the size of a kitchen sink.

Farther on through thick, rank grasses, ferns, and mosses, the water collected. Fed by other springs, it spread and mingled with the pebbly granite and limestone. In one spot campers had dug out around several boulders, enlarging the natural pool.

On the downhill side of the pool, one of the rocks had seen duty as a wash slab. The remains of a bar of soap were glued to the rock near the waterline. I headed for that pool. I couldn't have heard Estelle if she'd been screaming in my ear. The fire was seeking out heavy fuel, roaring up the hillsides on either side of the campsite and heading toward the massive stands of pine and fir up the slope.

We sank into the water. Compared to the blast of heat from the fire, the water was almost cool. The pool was eighteen inches deep where we snuggled next to the rock. The swale formed a natural chimney, and it would take the smoke and the fire quickly past us and up the hill. That's what I hoped.

Finn had miscalculated. He'd started the fire too close to the campsite. If he'd been a better arsonist, he'd have waited until he was near the highway, so the blaze would have had time to reach fire-storm proportions by the time it got to us.

As it was, there wasn't much fuel in the campsite other than grass and limb wood. The fire raced upward, seeking the timber. I pulled my right arm up across my chest, wincing as the water touched the wound in my shoulder. I breathed through the soaked cloth of my shirt sleeve. My left arm was around Estelle, and I made sure my wet uniform sleeve covered her nose and mouth.

Like two forlorn trolls, we rested in the small pool. I had never felt so goddamned helpless. The smoke swirled around us and I coughed, pressing my head down into the wet cloth and squirming back against the rock. Estelle was quiet. She'd passed out again. That was all right. She'd miss the show.

A juniper tree exploded a hundred feet away, and I flinched. I cracked open one eye. The surface of the pool was turning light gray. I splashed water on us and pulled Estelle close, trying to find a pocket of half-clean air under the slight overhang of the rock. I focused my mind on H. T. Finn.

"JUST BREATHE IN," the voice said. The bedroom light was a uniform gray. The face in front of me a blur. He was trying to jam something over my nose and mouth. "Easy now, sir."

The rich smell of woodsmoke brought a moment of panic. At first I imagined I'd been pulled from my burning house.

Someone else shouted something, much too loud. I tried to suck my head in, like a hurt turtle. Nothing worked. Nothing was in order.

"We need to bring her out first," the voice said, and another mumbled something unintelligible. I closed my eyes and somewhere deep inside my skull a switch clicked. I jarred to consciousness and coughed violently. "Easy now. Just hold still."

I felt the mask repositioned on my face and opened my eyes. Like a long lens on a television camera, they focused first far away, on the smoking hillside.

The blaze had moved up the mountain, and its steady roar was like a freight train in the distance. I struggled to distinguish the face in front of me. There were several now and eager hands reaching down into our little pool of gray water.

"Be careful," I tried to say. I pushed the oxygen mask away. "Be careful," I said again, and this time I think he understood me.

"Looks like a head injury on this one," he said. Hands far more expert than mine cradled Estelle Reye's head—her hair now gray from ash, the strands caked and thick like fresh cement. She was lifted from the pool and placed on the backboard.

Someone wiped my face and with the curtain of ash removed I recognized faces. Sheriff Pat Tate was kneeling in the goddamned pool of water. A shout from up-canyon pulled him to his feet before I had a chance to say a word.

"Just take it easy," Tate said to me, and he charged away. I turned in panic. Estelle Reyes was already gone, her stretcher headed downhill. I flailed wildly, and what seemed like half a dozen hands provided support.

"I can stand," I croaked, knowing damn well that I couldn't. It must have been a hell of a sight as a gray ash-man rose from the pool. The EMTs weren't much interested in what I had to say about my own rescue. Someone messed with my right shoulder even as other hands arranged my bulk on the backboard.

I was strapped down like a crazy man trussed in a strait-jacket. I couldn't do anything but relax and enjoy the trip. That gave me some time to think, to try to put some of the pieces together.

The helicopter rested at the east end of the parking lot, a stone's throw from the highway. My nerves tensed. The canyon was narrow and the air currents would be squirrelly.

"Maybe just a ride to town in an ambulance would be safer," I muttered, but no one listened to me. My stretcher was secured in the Jet Ranger even as the turbines increased their whine and the rotors flashed.

Estelle's stretcher was on the opposite side of the machine, and I wanted the damn mask off so I could ask about her.

I tensed as the helicopter lifted, ducked its nose, rotated in place, and then sped south, thumping up and out of the canyon. I caught a glimpse of the pall of smoke that hung on the southwest side of Quebrada Mesa and extended up the face of the mountain to the north.

It banked smoothly away from the valley. We had already gained enough altitude to establish a direct course to Albuquerque, skimming the mesas and foot-hills.

I shifted position, trying to see who else was in the helicopter with us. It was impossible to see, impossible to hear or even sit up. I settled back, wondering if Francis Guzman was with Estelle. I was going to have a hell of a time trying to explain this mess to him.

# TWENTY-SIX

"How are we?" the nurse asked. I'd been staring at the ceiling of the ICU recovery room and hadn't heard her pad in. She smiled at me, a little bit predatory.

I cleared my throat. "We're okay," I said. "What time is it?"

She glanced at her watch. "A little after eight."

There were no tubes stuck in me, no clicking machines. That was a plus. "In the morning?"

"Yes," the nurse said. She was maybe forty-five, plain as a post, and looked like she had more important things to do elsewhere.

I raised a hand and rubbed my face. My skin felt thin and fragile. "I need to know about the injured deputy who came in on the same helicopter as me." I was about to give her the name, and my mind went blank. "Christ," I muttered and rubbed my eyes again. "Estelle," I said suddenly. "Estelle Reyes." I looked at the nurse. I couldn't read her name tag. "I need to know. I'd appreciate anything you can do."

She nodded. "I'll see what I can find out." She left the room, and I twisted in bed just a little. My right shoulder felt heavy and dull, but when I bent the arm at the elbow everything worked. I looked at my fingers. Other than some minor nicks and cuts, every finger was in place and worked on command. Hell, this wasn't too bad, then.

I flexed my right leg. I couldn't see it over my belly, but it felt like all parts were in place. My right ankle twanged a bolt of lightning when I tried to point my toes.

In a few minutes the nurse returned. "The young lady is still in surgery," she said without preamble. My spirits sank.

"Is Dr. Francis Guzman in the building?"

"He may be in surgery, sir."

"I need to see him as soon as he's free."

"I'll see what I can do." She left again. The room was insulated from the normal sounds of the hospital, and I had only my thoughts for company. The door of the recovery room opened, and a uniformed sheriff's deputy poked his head in.

"Come on in."

"You're awake," he said. I saw by his uniform that he was one of Pat Tate's troops.

"I think so," I said.

"I've been assigned down here," he said, not altogether happy about it. "Sheriff Tate said that if there was anything you needed to let me know."

"There's a whole list of things I need," I said, eager to rejoin the world. "What's your name, Officer?"

"Perry Olguin, sir." He hadn't crossed thirty yet and was shorter than the nurse—slender, dark-skinned, and hawk-featured. He was cultivating a pencil-line mustache that looked ridiculous.

"Perry, catch me up. What the hell is happening up in San Estevan?"

Olguin frowned. "It's a mess, sir."

"Did they get Finn?"

"No, sir."

I took a deep breath. "So what happened? What about Al Martinez?"

"All I heard was that Finn took Al's car."

"Took his car? What about Al?"

"He'll be all right. His room's just down the hall. Finn somehow got the drop on him and shot him point-blank five times."

"And he's all right?"

"Well, he's sure sore. He had on his vest and I guess Finn didn't notice...or see it. Al's bruised up pretty bad. He can't breathe so good. He's lucky."

"Christ. Did he manage to get a radio call off?"

Olguin nodded. "He radioed in that shots were fired. He told me a few minutes ago that it sounded like a damn war."

"Worse," I said flatly. "Does Tate know what direction Finn went? How he went?"

Olguin frowned again. Maybe he had to do that in order to think. "They got a roadblock on State 46, sir. They're sure he didn't make it that far."

"What makes them think he's going to drive right down the state highway for Christ's sake?"

"Well...they've got every other road blocked, too. And the last word I had was that they were using two helicopters. It's kind of tough working north and east, though, because of the fire."

"He's not going north or east," I said. "That wouldn't make any sense."

"Yes, sir."

"How long did it take after Martinez's call before the next officers arrived?"

"Just a few minutes...maybe forty or so. Deputy

Polk was at the southern end of State 46. He sailed on up there pretty fast. And he didn't see any south-bound traffic."

And after the deputy went through it was an open road until they knew what the hell was going on and set up the roadblock. Whatever the screw-up had been, it was more our fault than Tate's. "And he switched cars, so he's not going to outrun anybody."

"They found Martinez's patrol car, you mean?"

"Yes, sir."

"Where was it? Where'd he dump it?"

Olguin paused and frowned even deeper. "They didn't say, sir. They're not talkin' about that on the radio."

"Shit," I said. It was after eight. In three or four hours Finn could easily be out of the state if he headed west or swung back around north. Or he could follow the labyrinth of dirt roads, gradually working his way south toward the Mexican border. "And Estelle Reyes is still in surgery?"

"Yes, sir."

"They recovered Paul Garcia's body?"

"Yes, sir."

"And nobody else is hurt? Other than Martinez, I mean?"

Olguin shook his head. Finn—that slimy son of a bitch—was loose and running, and none of us knew where he was.

"Is the fire under control?"

Olguin shook his head again. "That's going to be a bad one, sir. I heard on the radio that the wind's pick-ing up. And the fire's in heavy timber, movin' up the mountain. They got crews from all around the state, tryin' to stop it before it jumps across into the wilderness area on the north side."

I nodded, but it wasn't the forest fire I cared about. "Is Tate still at the hot springs?"

"Yes, sir."

"Get hold of him on the goddamn radio and tell him I need to talk to him."

"You can reach one of the deputies down at the campground parking lot. The repeater reaches in there. They can patch through on hand-held to the sheriff up the canyon."

"I know how radios work, Deputy," I snapped and immediately waved a hand in apology. "Look, I need to talk with Tate on a telephone, not the radio. Get through to him and have him find a phone. By the time he does that, I'll be out of here."

"Yes, sir."

Olguin left, and I reached for the buzzer to call a nurse. There was no buzzer. I swore loudly. The nurse showed up on the third curse.

"Is there something I can get for you?"

"Damn right," I said. "I need a telephone."

"There's no phone in here," she said, and I looked at her in disbelief.

"I know that, Nurse."

"I'll see one of the doctors. They may be ready to move you now."

"That would be nice." I smiled encouragement and then let my head fall back on the pillow. Estelle was in surgery, I was stuck in bed, and it sounded like Tate's men were either still mining the campsite or helping fight fires.

I hoped somebody was left to hound H. T. Finn's tail before little Daisy had to learn to speak Mexican.

# TWENTY-SEVEN

"HE DID WHAT?" I stared at Pat Tate.

The sheriff regarded me as if I'd given Finn the keys myself. Maybe that's why Tate had driven to the city instead of prolonging our phone conversation. "The son of a bitch parked Al Martinez's car right in Estelle's driveway. Then he broke a wing window of your Blazer and that was that."

"What the hell is that simple bastard up to?" I walked to the window. To the north, the plume of smoke towered like a summer thunderstorm's anvil—hell, airline pilots were probably smelling the pine smoke at 30,000 feet. "He won't be hard to find."

"No. There are probably only a thousand beat-up '84 Chevy Blazers in the state. But we got every road covered…one agency or another."

"And he's got Daisy with him."

"For sure," Tate said. "We saw the tracks of her little sneakers in the dirt of the driveway." He sat on the edge of the bed. His fingers twined together and he said quietly, "I don't believe we lost Paul. Twenty-two years old, for Christ's sake." He looked over at me, knowing there was nothing I could say that would make any difference. "We don't have any background on this guy yet, you know that?"

I nodded. Tate continued, "We're trying for a print match. What we need is one of those big computers that does that. We have the rifle and it might turn some prints. I think we recovered all the weapons, including that automatic of Arajanian's. It doesn't make sense that a punk kid like him can just plunk down a thousand bucks for a fancy gun and a goddamn silencer."

Tate looked at his watch. "I've got two investigators with Kyle Osuna right now," he said and then added with no sympathy, "That's one scared kid."

"He has reason to be."

"I was there for a few minutes and heard some of the preliminaries. You know why he wanted to talk with us so bad?"

"He was scared shitless, that's why."

"Partly. He was in the truck, all right, with the other four. He was up in the cab with Waquie and Kelly Grider. The Lucero brothers were in the back and he says they started the ruckus with the girl, almost the minute she climbed into the truck."

"They raped her?"

"Eventually, I guess. Osuna says they drove all the way to the head of the canyon to get some more beer at that little store…Chuga's. Then he says they went to one of the campgrounds up that way. Had themselves a party. By that time Cecilia Burgess was trying to get away—Osuna says she tried to run up into the woods and Kenneth Lucero caught her. Osuna says he tried to stop him, but Lucero was too much to handle."

"And after the party?"

"They drove south and Osuna said the girl was pleading with them to let her go, to drop her off when they got to the hot springs. He says they got to fighting in the back, with Waquie and Grider yelling encouragement from the front. Osuna says they were swerving all over the road."

"And he was lily-white innocent, of course."

"Sure. So he says. Somewhere north of the campgrounds, push came to shove. Osuna says that Kenneth Lucero lost his temper and hit the girl pretty hard. The truck swerved across the road, since Waquie was both drunk and enjoying the fight, not paying much attention to the road. He jerked the wheel at the wrong time and over she went."

"Osuna says the truck was southbound on the highway?"

"So he says. In the wrong lane."

"She gets tossed into the rocks and they drive on home."

Tate nodded. "More or less. But I have trouble with part of that punk's story. Osuna told the detectives that he went back up the canyon after a while in his own truck, found the girl, and helped her up to the highway. He says he would have done more, but then traffic came along and he spooked. He says he thought that since someone else was going to stop and take care of the girl, he could slip away."

"There's evidence that says that might be true, Pat. Both Estelle and I sure as hell thought it looked like someone had helped her up to the road. Maybe Osuna really did."

It was the first time during our conversation that Estelle's name had been mentioned, and Sheriff Pat Tate flinched perceptibly. He looked like he was ten years older than he was...physically tired and emotionally wrung out. He stood up and pushed one hand into his pocket, moving toward the door. He stopped and rested the other hand on the door pull, looking down at it thoughtfully.

"Al Martinez is fine. He's sore as hell, but fine. But we're not going to know anything about Estelle's condition until probably late this afternoon…maybe even tomorrow."

"I heard."

"If she pulls out of it, she's going to be one lucky girl."

I nodded and looked out the window. I wasn't sure I wanted Estelle to pull out of anything if she was going to face the rest of her life as a vegetable. No one had put that fear in words, but like a black cloud it hung over our thoughts.

Pat Tate turned and waited until I looked back at him. "Finn isn't going to get away with this, Bill." His heavy-lidded eyes didn't blink. "I wouldn't say this to anyone but you, but those punks in the truck had it coming. You and I both know they did. And that priest…Parris? He didn't know what the hell he was doing when he tipped off Finn." He shook his head in disgust. "But it's gnawing at me, what a cold, calculating bastard this Finn is. Hell, his girl got raped and smeared on the rocks. He flips out…I can almost understand that. I'd want to kill somebody myself. If he just walked up to each one of them and blew them away, that would be one thing. But the way he did it, Jesus. And he sure as hell didn't give you, Estelle, and Paul any notice. He just cut loose."

He stopped and rubbed the door pull with his thumb, idly polishing the chrome finish. "I'm surprised he gave you a second chance, Bill. When it comes to killing, he's no beginner."

"He used Arajanian," I said. "I'm sure of it. The boy did exactly as he was told. Cold-blooded as a goddamn lizard. I'm beginning to think that it's when Finn had to act on his own that he started making mistakes."

"I want to know what other connections he's had," Tate said. He pulled open the door. "We're going to find out who Finn is, Bill. And when we catch him, I'd straddle him over an anthill and let him take about three weeks to die, if the law would let me."

"Keep me posted," I said. He nodded and had almost closed the door behind him when my memory played a tape I didn't even know I had. "Pat!"

He peered back in the room and lifted his chin in question.

"When Finn came back to the tent, he picked up the little girl, Daisy."

"And?"

"He called her Ruth."

"Ruth?"

I nodded. "His pet name for her. I don't know why. The first time we talked with him at the springs, he called her that. Ruth. We didn't think it was important then. But now…it's something…it might lead somewhere."

Pat Tate frowned and I could see the wheels turning. No easy answer held up its hand. "When I find the son of a bitch, I'll ask him," he said.

"I want to be there when you do." He nodded and I took that as a promise.

# TWENTY-EIGHT

BY LATE AFTERNOON of the next day I was stir-crazy.
Worse, I hadn't seen Francis Guzman, hadn't heard
about Estelle…I was goddamned marooned in that
stupid little room. There was nothing wrong with me
other than a few stitches. "Admitted for observation"
might be a nice way of saying that I'd been sidelined
on purpose.

The manhunt for H. T. Finn was centering on the
western half of the state…it was top-of-the-hour news
on both radio and television and splattered a headline
across both the evening and morning papers. No reporter had sought me out. Sheriff Pat Tate had hidden
me away.

Shortly after 3:00 p.m., I was sitting in the hard
vinyl chair by the window of my hospital room. I'd had
a fitful night's sleep and, for want of anything better
to do, a short morning nap. The only medication they
forced on me was a mild painkiller and I took that
gladly. My back hurt worse than my shoulder.

The first rifle bullet had blown through my vest
and skinned across my back just below my shoulder
blades. The projectile had never broken the skin, but
the bruise and burn on my back was two inches wide
and nine inches long.

I'd been lucky with that one. The other bullet had
done more damage, ripping first through the edge of

my vest and then through the muscle over my right upper arm bone. The bullet hadn't actually hit the bone, although the shock wave had caused all kinds of "neurological confusion," as one of the doctors put it. An hour in surgery had put stitches in all the right places. One of the doctors told me that in two weeks I wouldn't even know I'd been nicked. Two weeks was forever.

There I sat, newspaper folded on my lap, looking ninety years old, when the door opened. Dr. Francis Guzman looked about as old as I did. And now that we were face-to-face, I wasn't sure I wanted to see him. He closed the door behind himself and leaned against it. He may have needed to. The bags under his eyes were black and deep.

I rose and he waved a hand at me. "No, don't. Sit."

"I've been doing nothing but sitting all day, Francis."

He pushed himself away from the door, walked slowly across the room, and shook my hand. His grip was firm and he hung onto my hand for just a moment. "How's the shoulder?"

"Fine. What's the word?"

He grinned—barely that…just a weary twitch of the lips and a little dance of light in his eyes.

"I'm sorry I haven't had a chance to get up here more often to see you," he said. "I looked in on you a couple times yesterday, but you were either under the anesthetic or asleep. Sheriff Tate told me last night you were getting antsy." He grinned. "I dropped in this morning and you were sleeping in that chair."

"Yeah. The hell with that. How's Estelle?"

"She's doing as well as we could hope."

He started to say something else, but he was sounding just like a goddamned doctor. I interrupted him.

"That doesn't mean a damn thing to me, Francis. Just tell me in simple English."

"She's going to live, barring complications."

"Complications?" Francis looked around the room for something to sit on. "Take the bed," I said. He flopped down and fell back, arms over his head. After a moment he pulled himself up to a sitting position.

"Whenever the brain is injured, there's all kinds of problems," he said. "It's a hell of a lot harder making sure all the bleeders behave themselves." He pointed his finger as if it were a pistol. "Apparently the bullet hit the point of her skull right here." He tapped the rear crown of his head. "A glancing blow, but..." He took a deep breath. "With a high-powered rifle there's just so damn much force involved. She has a serious skull fracture."

I waited while he decided what he wanted to say. "At first they thought that some skull fragments might have penetrated the dura, maybe damaged the brain tissue itself."

"And?"

"She was in surgery a long time. She's strong, and the docs did a fine job. The wound is clean. No chips. Hell of a lot of bruising, and that's always worrisome with the brain. But they did a fine job." He grinned with a little more energy. "I was there to make sure they did."

"Any paralysis?" I said, and my voice was husky.

He shook his head. "Not that we can tell yet."

"Is she conscious?"

"In and out, but that's to be expected for a couple days."

"I'd like to see her."

Francis Guzman nodded but held up a hand. "It'd be best for both of you to let it wait until tomorrow." He stood up and rolled his head around, trying to loosen the neck kinks. "Give her a few more hours of rest. We'll know more then, anyway."

"Francis…"

He looked at me, one eyebrow cocked—just like his wife. "What about the baby?"

The young physician smiled, and my relief was like ocean surf. "She told you, huh, Padrino?"

"Yeah, she told me. She didn't lose it, did she?"

"No. She'll be fine. Tough stuff. She really is."

"I'm sorry this happened," I said, sounding lame and dumb.

"Hindsight is a wonderful thing," he said. He stuck out his hand again, and I got up. "We'd all be geniuses if our foresight was as good. Who knows what might have happened if you'd waited. But she'll be fine. So will you. And the next time you have a vacation, we're all going to go to Lake Tahoe or somewhere where neither one of you can get into trouble."

"It's a deal." His spirits sounded upbeat, but I knew he was working at it. I followed him to the door, my shuffle just about as fast as his.

"And by the way…remember Nolan Parris?" Francis asked.

"Uh-huh."

"He's downstairs in one of the reading rooms. They won't let him up. He spent the night, I guess. But Tate set some tight rules on this one. Takes an act of Congress to see anyone or find out anything. You want to see him?"

"I don't know if I do or not."

"As I said, he spent the night. He must be pretty worried. Nobody's talking and he's concerned about the little girl. He means well, I think."

"Yeah," I said. "Finally, he's worried. We all are. But I don't know what it would accomplish to see him or..." and I stopped. My brain was beginning to work. I shrugged like I was making a hell of a concession. "Yeah. Send him up. No, wait. Forget it. I'll take care of it. I've got a phone."

Francis nodded. "I'll try to drop in on you later this evening. Behave yourself." He smiled.

"And you get some rest, kid. You look like shit." It felt good to be able to tell someone else that for a change.

Dr. Francis Guzman left, and I called the hospital gestapo to ask them if they'd let Father Nolan Parris enter the "R" zone. I had no desire to hash over his problems or his guilt that was no doubt rampaging after what had happened. It was simpler than that. I needed wheels, and Parris had access to a station wagon.

Age sixty-two is too late to worry about growing up and following the rules. There wasn't anything wrong with me that wouldn't heal as well elsewhere...where I might be more useful.

Nolan Parris hadn't found his way through the multilevel labyrinth to my room when the telephone rang. I grabbed it. It was Tate. The old bastard must have been a mind reader.

"Bill, are you dressed?"

"Hell, no. I'm sitting here in a goddamn robe pretending I'm a nursing home patient. What's up?"

"We got a break. A private pilot who was going to

fly over and look at the forest fire says he saw Finn's Blazer on one of the back roads of the reservation."

"It's not Finn's goddamned Blazer and where was this? Which reservation?"

"Northwest of Grants somewhere…over by Haystack Mesa, they called it. He's cornered at an old wildcat uranium mine. There's dozens of them out that way. We've got it pinpointed on the map. A chopper is going to pick me up here in a minute."

I was about to interrupt him and tell him that if I got left out of this one I'd curse his firstborn for generations. But there was a light knock on my door, and Nolan Parris stepped into the room. He was wearing his clerical suit, complete with white collar. I turned my attention back to the telephone.

"You have to pick me up, Pat."

"That's why I called. I cleared it with the hospital already. You need to get your old ass in gear, get dressed, and be at the helipad on the roof in about thirty minutes."

"You got it."

"And, Bill…"

"Yep?" I was already impatient to be off the phone.

"I'm not doing this as a favor to you. I want you to know that from the start. If it was up to me, you'd be locked in that hospital room for a week or so. I'm doing it because I was told to do it."

I slammed on the brakes. I couldn't imagine Pat Tate taking orders from anyone. "This is your case, Pat."

"Damn right it's my case. And it's going to stay that way. But he's got the child and this may be our only chance." I heard the steady whup-whup of a helicopter in the background, and someone shouted at Tate.

"I'll talk with you in a few minutes. Finn must know he's not going to slip through the net. He's cornered, Bill. And he knows it. Now he wants to talk to you."

"Finn wants to talk to…"

"Thirty minutes, Bill. Don't make us wait." Tate hung up and I stared out the window, the phone still in my hand. If the media had pried enough information out of Tate to know that the hospital was treating two survivors from the war on the mountain, Finn would have heard the news on any radio station. He knew my face. If he'd rifled through the glove compartment of the Blazer, he knew my name. The bastard wanted to negotiate.

I had forgotten that anyone else was in the room. Nolan Parris had heard enough though.

"Sheriff," he said, and I turned around to look at him.

"You have to let me go along." Parris limped across the room and touched my arm. He repeated his request, and I hung up the phone and pushed myself out of the chair.

"Why the hell not," I said. If another passenger on the helicopter was all right with Pat Tate, it was fine with me. I didn't know how they'd managed to corner the son of a bitch, but the rules had changed. Maybe the services of a priest would be useful.

# TWENTY-NINE

FLOYD'S NUMBER TWO was a vertical shaft sunk into the bleak, tan desert just off one corner of the Navajo reservation. The boneyard around the mine was littered with three decades of rusting hardware and trash.

By the time our helicopter arrived, there were five cops for every lizard.

H. T. Finn had taken the wrong turn. The two-track had swerved around an abrupt rise and then dead-ended at the mine headframe. My Blazer had been spotted earlier by a private pilot as the truck kicked up a plume of dust, heading west. The pilot had called the cops. A customs helicopter had given chase then ran out of fuel. They'd skipped back to Gallup, figuring it was either that or walk. If they'd stuck on Finn's ass another minute, they'd have had him.

"In a day and a half, Finn could have been deep in Mexico, if he'd dodged all the right roadblocks!" I shouted at Tate over the noise of the chopper. "This is only a hundred miles from San Estevan, as the crow flies!"

Tate pointed at my Blazer and I had my answer. A long, jagged rent tore the bodywork from the driver's door back to the bumper. From where I stood I could see that Finn had had to mount the spare tire, a ratty summer tread two sizes smaller than the rest.

He'd tangled with something. Too bad it hadn't

ripped his goddamn arms off. If Daisy had been hurt, I'd rip his arms off.

We made our way through the flying dirt and dust to the old headframe. I ignored all the curious faces except one.

I knew Sheriff Edwin Sterns from days gone by—felons rarely bother to observe county lines, and over the years a cop meets his compadres from other agencies. This county was Sterns's—and it fitted him, big, lazy, and all but empty.

He was a tall, gangly man with a potbelly that looked like he was carrying a bedpan under his shirt. He'd been a state trooper years before but had found their military bearing too much trouble to imitate.

"How'd you rope this one, Gastner?" he asked as we shook hands. "And what the hell brings you all the way north into God's country?"

"Just lucky."

Tate said, "He's on vacation."

Sterns shook his head in wonder. "Hell of a vacation." He turned and motioned us over to the headframe.

The mine shaft gaped, the opening ten feet square. The damn hole went straight down into the earth. The shaft's edges were heavily timbered, and a thin grating of woven steel like the troops used to make runways over soggy ground in Vietnam covered the opening. The mesh rested on an H-frame of two-inch angle iron. At one time a barbed-wire fence had enclosed the area, but now that was broken and scattered. I shuffled carefully to the edge and looked down. The shaft was bottomless black.

Directly across from where I stood, a corner of the

mesh had been pried up. Below the torn mesh, a steel ladder disappeared into the depths. The ladder hugged the wall of the shaft, the rungs no more than four inches from the timbers to which the ladder frame was bolted. There was no safety cage around the ladder. Once a man was on his way down, there was no other support if his hands should slip from the rust-covered, half-inch-diameter rungs…just a lot of empty space. It gave me the willies.

"And he's down in there? With the child?"

"Sure as hell," Sterns said.

I wasn't a bit surprised that no one had followed Finn down inside that hole.

"We've got to get Daisy out of there," Parris said. His eyes were wild, and I took him by the arm. He looked like he wanted to step out on the mesh.

"Shit," I said and looked westward. "If it was me, I'd rather take my chances walking out across the desert than sliding down in that hole. And he had my Blazer, for God's sakes. He could have kept going, road or no road."

"Maybe he figured he was cornered," Tate said. "Maybe he didn't know the chopper had to call it off."

Sterns shoved his hands in his pockets. "He asked for you, Gastner. My guess is that he thinks you're his ticket. And while he waits, he's sure as hell safe here. Nobody's going to sneak up behind him."

I turned away from the hole. I kept my grip on Parris's arm, pulling him with me like a wayward child. "How the hell deep is that thing?"

Sterns stepped right to the edge and looked down through the wire mesh. "I'd guess five, six hundred feet. Maybe more. We're lookin' to find Stubby Begay.

He's a Navajo who lives in these parts. He used to work for Simon-Yates, and one of the deputies said he thinks Begay was on the crew that used to work this hole." Chances were nil anyone would have a blueprint of the mine…and if they did, it'd take a week to get it.

"Let's check the truck," I said. "See what the son of a bitch took. Maybe he took the handheld radio down into the shaft with him." I turned to one of the deputies. "Stay with this man," I told him and hauled Parris around within reach of the deputy.

The Blazer wasn't locked and the keys were in the ignition. I glanced in the back. "The bastard went camping," I said. "He took my sleeping bag." I peered under the driver's seat. "And the radio." I rummaged some more. "And a .45 automatic I kept stowed here."

I straightened up and rested my forearms on the seat cushion. Lying on the passenger seat was the wad of newspaper that had been under the seat, serving as a cushion for the radio. I frowned. I was not an overly neat individual when it came to housekeeping—but now the newspapers had been folded with care. The two-week-old Albuquerque paper was on top, with a quarter of the front page torn off. The tear went through the middle of some notes I'd scribbled in the margin.

I remained motionless, lost in thought. What the son of a bitch was up to was a mystery to me. Hell, I had no idea whether a hand-held radio even worked underground…or for that matter if the batteries in mine were charged.

I reached over and snapped open the glove compartment. I couldn't tell if my mess in there had been rearranged, but nothing appeared to be missing. I shook my head.

The Blazer's two-way radio was an old-fashioned Motorola, and when I turned on the ignition I saw it still worked. So did the gas gauge. The needle rested below "E."

The Motorola was set on channel one, car-to-car. I hefted the mike. "Finn, do you hear me?" Pat Tate had walked around to the other side of the Blazer, and he leaned against the door. I repeated the call. A short burst of static crackled over the speaker, sounding faint. A try on the other channels produced nothing.

"He either don't have the radio on or it don't work underground," Tate said.

"I've never been down in a mine. I don't know." I hung up the microphone and switched off the ignition. "Finn doesn't know me from a hole in the head," I said. "He met me that first time Estelle and I walked up to the camp." That seemed years before. "If he drove your deputy's car to the Guzman's house and took my truck, then he was planning ahead. How the hell did he know about the Blazer?"

A deputy started to walk toward us and Tate waved him off. "Maybe he didn't. He knew who Estelle was and without a doubt knew who Francis was…especially if the Burgess girl had occasion to visit the clinic. Hell, if you live in a dinky town like San Estevan, you know everybody sooner or later. Maybe he knew about Dr. Guzman's Isuzu four by four and was after that. Guzman wasn't home so he settles for yours. And you got to figure, the way things went down, yours was about the only one he'd be able to take without worrying about the owner showing up."

"Maybe."

"Another possibility is that the night Osuna was shot

Arajanian followed him to the Guzmans', hoping for another try. He sees you and spooks." He shrugged. "So he tells Finn about it when he gets back. He had the time. If Arajanian watched you load Osuna into the Blazer, it makes sense he'd tell Finn about that, too."

I didn't much like the notion that while Estelle and I had been helping the wounded Osuna the creep with the silenced Beretta had been lounging around outside the adobe house, watching our every move—with his finger itching on the trigger.

If that had been the case, he could have taken us all out, then and there. Whatever he'd been, maybe he hadn't been a creative little bastard. He'd needed instructions from his boss.

As we walked back toward the shaft, I saw that the crowd was growing. I gestured at Sterns, and he broke away from a powwow he was having with a couple of men in business suits.

"You have a bullhorn? A hailer?" I asked.

"Sure. I mean, I'm sure somebody does." Sterns turned and shouted at one of his deputies. The kid produced one of those little battery-powered amplifiers that track coaches love. I took it and walked to the shaft. Another helicopter roared overhead, and I glanced up. It was one of the television stations.

"Sheriff, you need to rope this place off before the crowd gets so thick someone knocks me into the mine shaft," I told Sterns, and the sheriff assigned that project to three of the deputies who were underfoot.

They charged off, one of them with his M-16 at high port like he'd been ordered to take a hill.

I took my time. I dug the bell of the bullhorn into the sand and lowered myself to my knees. I could smell the stale air of the mine as I leaned over the mesh. I knew my head and shoulders were silhouetted against the sky if Finn should be down in the shaft looking up.

I switched on the horn and pressed the trigger. "Finn...are you listening?"

"I have to talk with Daisy," Parris said, again at my elbow. I ignored him, trying to hear some response from down under.

"Finn!" I yelled. My words bounced around the guts of the mine shaft. He was going to have to shout to be heard over the cars, helicopters, and yakking that was going on behind me, but I was sure there'd been no response.

I was lifting the bullhorn for a third try when I heard his voice, distant but clear as crystal.

"Send Gastner."

I glanced at Tate then triggered the hailer. "This is Gastner. I'm listening."

"I want to talk to you."

"So talk."

I didn't understand what he said next and I turned to Sterns and snapped, "If those sons a bitches can't keep quiet, arrest 'em, goddamn it. We're trying to conduct some business here."

"Finn, I didn't understand you."

He exaggerated each word with a pause between each. "Face...to...face."

"Come on up and we'll do that."

"Down...here."

"Oh, sure," I said without turning on the bullhorn. I triggered it and added, "That's not possible."

"Make...it...possible."

Parris was fidgeting and I said, "Do you have the little girl with you?"

"And…she…will…remain…with…me."

"He can't do that," Parris said and his voice shook.

"Be quiet," I said and then keyed the hailer. "Is she safe?"

"Yes."

"Then let us bring her up. You won't be harmed."

A sound that could have been a laugh floated up. "There…is…only…one…choice. You…meet…me…face…to…face…down…here."

"Don't be a fool. I can't climb down the ladder."

Tate leaned over a little, looking down. He said quietly, "If he gets on that ladder with the kid, there's no way he can defend himself."

I had visions of Daisy pinwheeling like a broken doll down into the depths of the old mine. "He'll use the girl as a shield."

"Sure," Sterns said. "And when he gets up here and steps away from the edge, one rifle bullet through the head, he's dead, and the girl's safe."

I didn't like the sound of that either. I hefted the hailer again. "Finn—you have to let the girl go. Let us send an unarmed deputy down to bring her up."

"No. Ruth…is…the…answer. She…remains…with…me."

"What the hell is he talking about?"

"I don't know. He calls her Ruth. Who the hell knows why." I hefted the bullhorn. "Finn, nobody is going to hurt either you or the girl if you give yourself up."

"Tell…Robert…that."

"He means Arajanian," I said to Tate. "That's over, Finn. Come on up."

"No. Face…to…face…with…you." There was a pause. "And…you…know…why."

I looked at Tate and said, "I do?"

The sheriff shrugged. "This guy's a fruitcake."

Apparently we hadn't responded promptly enough, because Finn's voice floated up. "Don't…play… games…Mister…Sheriff."

"Finn, if you don't send the girl up, we're going to have to come down and get her. You know what that means."

He knew I was bluffing. There wasn't a drop of concern in his tone when he said, "Don't…be…a…fool." That calm, detached voice floating up out of the ground was enough to raise goose bumps. I sat back on my haunches. My shoulder hurt. My right ankle throbbed. I eyed the ladder. There was no way I could climb down that with only one good arm. Hell, if nothing else, my belly would throw me off balance and there I'd go.

"Any ideas?" I asked Tate. "You want to go down?"

"Don't be ridiculous. There's no way I can climb down there."

Sterns was eager. "We can lower you somehow. Use one of those ass slings like the search and rescue uses. One of my deputies is up on that stuff."

"Um," I said. I glanced at the hole. One of the deputies trotted toward us, his boots raising dust. Everyone else had been herded well away, behind the yellow plastic banner that ran from car bumper to bumper.

"Sir," he said, "they found Mr. Begay. They'll be here in just a few minutes."

"All right," I said. "Let's find out what this hole

looks like before we jump in it. See if we have any options." I raised the bullhorn and said, "Finn, we're going to find a way to get me down there. Give us some time."

"Nothing…but…time," he replied.

"That goddamned cocky son of a bitch," I said. "Find me an elevator," I said to Sterns, "and you're probably going to need about a mile of 2,000-pound test rope. By the time you find that, we'll have Begay… and one more thing. I want a small automatic with a good silencer." Sterns looked puzzled.

"Bill's right," Tate said. "If you had to fire a gun down in that mine, the whole thing's apt to collapse."

"I'm going with you," Parris said. I regarded him for a second.

His face was covered with sweat and he looked like he was ready to faint.

"No," I said flatly. I didn't have either time or inclination to baby-sit. I motioned to one of the deputies. "Find him some shade somewhere." I turned back to Sterns. "I'm not going down there unarmed," I said. "Finn's a master of one-way deals. And it's not going to happen again."

"We've got Arajanian's Beretta in Albuquerque," Tate said. "It's in the evidence locker. You kept a hold on that through thick and thin."

"Too big. I want something small…something that I can hide. I won't use it unless I can get close enough to shove it up his ass."

"Well, I'll work on that," Sterns said. He walked off, scratching his head.

Tate glanced at me. He didn't have much faith in Edwin Sterns. "I know someone in Albuquerque who can get us anything we need. We'll send one of the choppers in for it."

I nodded and he gestured to his detective. For a moment I was alone at the rim of the shaft. I looked down into the hole and felt a chill.

# THIRTY

STUBBY BEGAY ARRIVED about six-thirty—a short, scrawny man with badly bowed legs, a narrow, hawk-nosed face, and stone-black eyes. He had two teeth left, one snaggled right in front of his tongue so that he lisped. He talked so softly that in order to hear him I had to hunker down with him, his face no more than a foot from mine as he drew pictures in the dust.

According to Begay the vertical shaft of Floyd's Number Two sank 785 feet below the headframe. We tested the depth with dinner.

Earlier Finn had agreed that we could send food down for the little girl. We considered spiking the food to put them both out, but I knew damn well that Finn wouldn't fall for something that simple. And we had no way of knowing who might eat what…a dose necessary to knock out Finn would kill Daisy. So we played it straight. The small plastic cooler of sandwiches, fruit, and milk sank out of sight. The hundred yards of chalk line that we knotted to the cooler's handle ran out and was tied to another ball of brown twine, and that reeled off for what seemed forever. Every inch of that 785 feet paid out before the cooler touched bottom.

We waited several minutes and then we heard Finn shout, "Pull…it…out!" We did so. There was no way we could touch the son of a bitch.

Begay enlarged his drawing in the dirt. "You got a

drift on that side at 300 feet," Begay said. "It's an old pump station. And here, at 430, and another here, at 785. Right on the bottom."

"Side tunnels, you mean?"

"They call 'em drifts." His eyes twinkled.

"That's where he must be then," I said, tapping the bottom.

"I'd be right here," Begay said and gouged his stick into the sand where he'd sketched the first side tunnel, or drift, 300 feet down.

"Why's that?"

"'Cause the ladder goes right by it. No need to go to the bottom."

"The food went all the way down."

Stubby Begay grinned. His gums looked like plastic. "So you think he's on the bottom." He grinned even wider. "He takes the string and…" He made hand-over-hand motions as if he were pulling a bundle up. "He fake you out good that way."

I frowned. "What about the other drifts? The deeper ones?" He shrugged.

"There's no way to reach them other than the ladder?"

Begay shook his head. "If it ain't come loose."

I looked up at Tate and Sterns. "Maybe that explains why we can hear him so well when he shouts," I said. "If he's only a hundred yards down in that first drift."

"Only," Tate said. He turned and watched two of the deputies unloading gear from the trunk of one of the patrol cars.

"So, Stubby, how about this. If I was lowered down in a sling seat, right along the ladder, I'd fetch up at this drift." I tapped the dirt. "Where you say he's got to be."

"That's what I say."

"There's nowhere else he might be?" Begay shrugged. "I mean except maybe the other side tunnels." He shook his head.

I looked over at the climbing harness that one of the deputies was shaking loose. "There's enough rope there?"

"Plenty," Sterns said. He sounded confident. It wasn't his ass in the sling.

As we made final preparations, the sun set. Spotlights from three cars converged on the shaft entrance, bathing it in harsh white light. Two big four-wheel-drive pickups had been recruited and parked thirty feet away, facing the shaft. Their floodlights added to the artificial daylight. The deputies attached the ropes to both front axles. They knew their job and took their time. When everything was finally ready, it was dark outside the circle of spotlights.

I looked down into the shaft, skeptical. The rope had to let me down right along the ladder so I could keep my feet planted and be able to use my one good arm. Otherwise, I'd just dangle and spin in the shaft, nothing more than a target on a string. The two deputies repositioned one of the trucks and were confident. I wasn't.

"Sir?" The deputy, Gareth Burns, gestured for me. "Can you step into this?" He held up a bright blue nylon harness that looked like a big athletic supporter.

With several sets of hands assisting, I was trussed up tight enough to choke. Then two big steel rings were clipped into the nylon loops in front.

"Can you work these with one hand?" the deputy asked. He gave me a demonstration of how the carabiner worked and then watched me diddle with the lock ring. I pressed in the release and the ring came off. "Good. Although you might just want to leave it hooked up. We can pay out all the rope you'll need."

"Terrific."

He nodded, mistaking my grimace for enthusiasm. "And I'll just clip these two other harnesses to the belt here, so when it comes time to bring everybody up, we can do it right." He had different plans than I did.

They pushed a plastic hard hat with a miner's light on my head and pulled the chinstrap tight.

At one point during the preparations, Pat Tate handed me a tiny Colt .380 automatic. The silencer looked like a six-ounce juice can. I handed it back to him. "Put a round in the chamber."

"You sure?"

"Yes, I'm sure." After he did so, I pointed the muzzle of the gun off into the desert. The tiny safety catch was awkward to use with my left hand. I practiced snapping it on and off, then slid the little pistol inside my shirt, sticking its snout under the bandages that bound my right shoulder, arm, and ribs.

"Is that going to work?" Pat Tate asked.

"It's going to have to," I said. Pat didn't ask what my plans were. The deputy snapped another large flashlight to my belt. It hung from a nylon loop.

"Slide this in your hip pocket," Tate said and held out a slender black penlight.

The deputy saw my expression at the third light. "Rule of threes," he said. "It's dark down there." I didn't argue. Tate adjusted the hand-held radio in its holster and made sure the microphone cord was free. The mike was clipped to my collar. I felt like a goddamned hardware store, but we were as ready as we could be.

Sterns jerked a thumb in the direction of the crowd. "The television station sure would like to be able to bring their cameras on over," he said.

"Sure," I said. He looked hopeful. "On one condition."

"What's that?"

"That you be the one to go down there."

He didn't like that much, but he didn't mention the news hounds again.

I picked up the hailer. "Finn! I coming down now."

"Take…your…time."

I handed the hailer to Tate. "Polite bastard, isn't he?"

The deputies handled me like glass. The iron mesh and its frame had been pulled completely off the shaft opening, and the hole gaped ominously. I stood with my back to the hole, the ladder's top rung behind me.

"Now just lean a little against the rope so your weight is diggin' in your heels," the deputy said. "And remember with this Z-haul, you're goin' down in five- or six-foot bites. We'll keep 'er just as smooth as we can. Now just edge on back until you got your feet on the ladder."

The deputy had his hand on my left elbow while another adjusted a set of heavy edge rollers to guide the rope. I waited patiently, my pulse pounding in my ears.

"Just trust the rope," Burns said.

"Do I have a choice?" I replied.

"Really, it works easy as can be. Now, just step down. Real easy. Leave it up to the rope." I did so while he orchestrated. The ladder flexed and I stopped. "Go on down until you can hang onto the top rung," he said.

One awkward step at a time, I backed down the ladder. After four rungs, I grabbed the ancient rust of the top rung in my hand.

"Now just relax for a minute and sit in the sling."

He switched his light back and forth, checking ropes. The weight was off my feet, and with a twitch of the hand I could have spun around like a kid on one of those swings made out of an old tire. I kept my feet on the ladder rungs and my hand in place.

I twisted my head and looked down. The pencil beam from my helmet light shot down into the darkness. I looked up and squinted against the glare of the spotlights. Pat Tate was standing close by, as was Sterns. Both of them had that look on their faces that said, "Better you than me, kid."

I took a deep breath. "All right," I said. "Let's get this over with."

# THIRTY-ONE

SIX FEET AT A TIME, I sank into the earth. I kept my feet free of the ladder, learning to trust the sit-harness. The ladder's iron side rail slid through my left hand. That small contact was my anchor.

The vertical sides of the shaft were timbered, and in more than one spot water dripped down the face of the wood. The timbers smelled musty. I wondered what pockets of gases waited down below, trapped by the years of stagnation. I'd heard stories about miners walking into shafts where they took a breath and keeled over before they had time to turn around. That couldn't be the case here…Finn had no shortage of breath.

As the bright light of the entrance drifted up and away, the shaft seemed to narrow with me at its focus. My mind played games with the perspective. When I was fifty feet down, the deputy touched me with the beam of his flashlight.

"Any problems?" he asked. He didn't bother with the radio.

"No," I said. The rope played out again. The next time I looked up, I flinched. I could have covered the opening of the mine with the palm of my hand. Looking down, I saw the beam from my helmet light stab into nothing. No bottom. Just wooden timbers and old iron.

I avoided looking at the rope. What on the surface had looked stout and unbreakable in its coil now stretched out above me thin and gossamer. Every time the deputies reached the end of a pulley bite and the drop stopped, the rope twanged from side to side slightly.

On impulse I reached up and turned off my helmet light. The blackness of the mine was complete, the entrance above nothing but an insignificant postage stamp of artificial light. I caught my breath as the rope descended again. The light had been my lifeline to equilibrium and I turned it back on.

The side tunnel, what Stubby Begay had called a drift, took me by surprise. The side of the shaft had been passing by my left shoulder as I descended, a steady, unchanging parade of old wood timbers, dripping water, and abandoned iron fittings. I hadn't used the side of the shaft for support. Nevertheless, when it suddenly shelved inward, away from me, my stomach tightened. The rope dropped me far enough that my light shot into the tunnel.

The drift was nearly as large as the main shaft. I breathed in relief at seeing something substantial and horizontal.

I turned my head slightly, keyed with my left hand, and spoke into the hand-held radio's mike that was clipped to my shirt collar.

"Stop," I said. "I'm at the drift."

"Affirmative."

I pushed away from the ladder, rotating to face the drift. The floor of the tunnel was littered with junk— old sections of pipe, fittings, various lengths of wire and cable. The light illuminated heavy timbers and a series of three small concrete pads, each two feet high.

Rusted bolts thrust up from the concrete where at one time machines had been secured.

Stubby Begay had called it a pump station. The miners hadn't left much behind…just enough scars and litter to puzzle archaeologists in another thousand years.

For the first thirty feet the drift was as securely timbered as the main shaft. But forty feet back the drift elbowed to the left and the timber supports ended. I couldn't see around the bend. The place made my skin crawl.

Rotten and water-soaked as the timbers were, they gave the illusion of strength and support. In the drift they gave way to something that looked like monstrous cobwebs, with patches of the material hanging down from a ceiling of jagged rock. It was some sort of fabric, bolted right to the face of the shaft.

In dozens of places rock fragments littered the floor of the drift where the old fabric had pulled loose, and off to the left, just visible before the drift turned out of sight, an entire section of wall and ceiling had slumped, filling nearly a third of the tunnel.

I swept the light carefully, looking for movement.

"Finn?" I said. My voice echoed down the shaft. The dust of the years had padded the floor, and the fresh tracks were as clear as if they had been painted on a sidewalk with Day-Glo paint. And the prints came in two sizes.

"Finn, are you in there?" Again my words rattled around and died with no response. I ducked my head and looked down the main shaft. Ten feet below the drift, the iron supports that held the ladder had pulled loose…or rusted through. The section of ladder was twisted away from the wall and hung off at an angle. Finn had to be in the drift.

I reached for the second flashlight, adding its beam to that of my helmet. I saw that with just a slight stretch I could plant my feet on the lip of the drift's shaft and grab one of the wall timbers with my left hand. With some slack in the rope I could pull myself into the tunnel.

If I slipped and fell, it would hurt like hell, but the rope could be trusted. That's what the deputy had said.

"Turn off your light," Finn said. His voice was quiet and conversational.

Out of reflex I swung the lights toward the sound of his voice. Nothing. I snapped off the flashlight and let it hang, then reached up and turned off my helmet. The blackness was oppressive...the spotlights above at the shaft mouth served only as a beacon in the distance. I reached up and touched the small, reassuring pistol grip of the Colt under my arm sling. I waited.

"Sheriff, you copy?" The crackle of the damn radio sounded like a string of firecrackers.

I keyed the mike and snapped, "Stay off the air."

"Ten-four."

I took a deep breath, my fingers still covering the lump that was the automatic. "All right, Finn. What do you want?"

Unless Finn had developed sonar, he could see no more than I. His light exploded out of the darkness, and I jerked my head back in surprise.

"Get that goddamned thing out of my eyes," I snapped, but he took his time. Finally the light slipped away and I cracked an eyelid. The beam was centered on the thick bandage that bound my right arm and shoulder. My right hand stuck out of the linen and lay flat against my belly, useless. Finn played the light this way and that, examining me and my equipment.

"Turn around," he said and watched as I touched the shaft wall with my fingers and gently pushed myself so that I rotated on the rope. The wash of his light cast a fat shadow of me on the opposite wall of the vertical shaft. As I rotated back around, he turned off the light. I blinked my eyes, trying to put out the yellow sunbursts that remained.

"So," he said.

"Are you through playing games? Where's the child?"

"She's asleep. And you've managed to make quite a name for yourself, haven't you? I underestimated your tenacity."

I was in no mood to exchange compliments. "You have to let us bring her up. Nobody's going to hurt her...or you."

Finn chuckled. "I can imagine." The harness dug into my crotch and belly, and my right leg was falling asleep. Finn knew he had all the time in the world. I didn't if I was to be worth anything.

"I was surprised that you had put it all together, Sheriff," he said.

I tried to picture where he might be standing. "Sometimes I get lucky."

"Yes," he said. "Had your truck not let me down, we wouldn't be having this conversation now."

"What do you want, Finn? What do you think I can do for you?" I was tired of hanging like a goddamned potted plant.

"I saw the newspapers under the seat. You're a clever

man, to make the association. I'm curious why you didn't call in any of the other authorities earlier."

I frowned and said, "What do..." when what he'd said hit me like a sledge, smashing open the doors of my rusty memory. The newspapers. My notes. Until this day, I'd last seen the papers Friday night when I parked at the campground. The two-week-old papers, one of them with the front page headline...my notes in the margin.

I breathed a silent curse. We'd received the bulletin from Washington State along with a thousand other law enforcement agencies. We were close to the border. It made sense.

H. T. Finn had seen the newspaper when he'd stolen the radio—the headline and my notes. He had assumed that I'd made the connection, knew who he was, what he'd done.

"Arajanian did those hits for you, too," I said, trying to keep my voice calm and hoping that he didn't recognize the guess.

"He learned well," Finn said. "He would have been of great use to me."

My mind raced. "No, he did just what you wanted," I said. "It worked out better the way it was...you left the rifle with him for the police to find. It's probably the same rifle you had him use on the governor of Washington and the prison warden, isn't it? If there was a matchup, it'd tie those shootings to the kid, and you'd be long gone. No witnesses to say otherwise after you shot us...and set the mountain on fire."

"Cleansing fire," Finn said softly, and his voice drifted off as he recited, "'And the fire shall cleanse the evil from the earth and...'" His voice became indistinct.

"And they don't know you as Finn in Washington, do they?" I said, but he refused the bait.

Finally he said, "You will make arrangements, Sheriff. Listen carefully." I wasn't in a position to do otherwise, but I wanted answers to a flood of questions. Finn continued, "I want a fully fueled helicopter. The television station has one. The helicopter, one reporter, and a pilot. That's all. It will land immediately beside the mouth of the shaft, close enough that I can see the flash of its blades over the opening."

I sighed. Why was an aircraft always such magic to these fruitcakes? Where would he go, other than Mexico? And what made him think Mexico would want him? He wanted a reporter, and that meant he thought the world would be interested in hearing his sorry tale.

My eyes ached with the strain of trying to see him in the darkness, and my finger itched to reach for the Colt automatic. But he had the girl, and we would play his game until the time was right.

"That's all?"

"As a beginning, yes."

"You'll let them send down two more ropes, one for the girl and one for you?"

"No!" he said sharply. "Ruth and I will use the ladder. We will go out the way we came in." He laughed softly. "You'd like me in harness, helpless. You'd like that, wouldn't you. Oh no. That's how they killed my Ruth. It won't happen again. Never again."

Another Ruth. But now it was the little girl I worried about. "It's a long climb. I was just trying to make it safe for Daisy."

"You don't need to be concerned. Just do as I say."

"All right."

"Talk to the ones on the surface now," he commanded.

I keyed the mike. "Gastner here."

"Go ahead, Gastner."

"Listen carefully, and get this right the first time. Finn wants Channel 8's Jet Ranger, fully fueled, with a pilot and a reporter on board. He wants it to set down immediately beside the mineshaft. We have to be able to see the blades flash, or he won't go for it. No one else in the way. The three of us will come up. The three of us will board the chopper. Is that understood?"

After a pause, I heard Pat Tate's voice. "Understand: Channel 8's chopper, one pilot, one reporter. They might not agree to that."

"Don't waste time, Pat." The television crew would leap at the chance to be evening news. "And nothing else. Tell everyone to keep their fingers off the damn triggers. I don't want the girl hurt."

"Ten-four. Search and rescue wants the girl in a harness, on a rope."

"No," Finn said loudly.

"Look," I said. "It's for her own safety, Finn. Use your head. You could slip. Without a harness, there's nothing between you and 400 feet of shaft."

His voice regained its original composure. "If you and your men do as I say, there won't be any slips, will there?"

"Gastner, did you copy?"

I keyed the mike. "Negative on the rope," I said. My brain raced. There was no way a four-year-old child was going to be carried up 300 feet of rusted, slippery ladder.

"We'll see what we can do," Tate said, and the shaft fell silent. I shifted in the harness, trying to let some blood down my right leg. "Finn, listen to me. Turn your light on." To my surprise he did so, keeping the beam centered on my torso. "Are you wearing a heavy belt?"

He didn't answer.

"Look, if you are, use this." I turned and groped with my left hand for the small harness that the deputy had clipped to my own. "They gave me this. Put it on Daisy, and clip her to your belt. At least do that."

"No." He turned off the light.

"Damn it, she'll be clipped to you. She'll be safe that way. What can we do if she's clipped to you? No one can make a move to grab her. And it keeps your arms free. It will be even better."

Finn was silent, and I hoped he was weighing his options. "All right," he said. "Throw the harness into the tunnel." He turned on the light. I breathed a sigh of relief. For several minutes I fumbled with the carabiner before the big steel ring snapped open. I tossed the smaller of the two extra harnesses into the drift.

The beam always fastened on me, Finn made his way through the scattered junk. He stopped when the line of pump foundations separated us. I couldn't tell if he held a weapon in his other hand. "Tell them to pull you up ten feet."

The bastard was shrewd. I keyed the mike and repeated his order. I had no sense of moving. Rather, the entrance of the drift sank, as if the wall itself slid downward. My feet were just above the top of the tunnel mouth when the pull stopped.

"Finn, do you know how to hook up that harness?

Do it properly now." I shouted, suddenly frantic at not being able to see inside the drift.

He didn't respond, but I heard his footfalls as he advanced and picked up the harness. I tried to picture him bending down, then straightening up, and then retreating back down the shaft. I counted eight footfalls, then lost him. There was no other time to take the gamble. I reached up and gently keyed the mike. I kept my voice a husky whisper.

"Don't answer," I whispered. "Give me five bites down." Their response was immediate. In the darkness I felt the wall slide by, felt the breath of air as the drift yawned in front of me. I'd have one chance. I stretched out my feet, my toes reaching for rock. The floor of the drift touched my left foot and I grabbed with my left hand, my teeth clenched.

I felt wood, slipped, and grabbed a rough crack in the timber. I yanked with all my strength, pulling the rope in after me. As the downward bite continued, I let my weight carry me into the drift until I was resting on my left hand and both knees. My right leg, until then sound asleep, tingled sharply with the new movement.

Above they would continue to pay out the rope, giving me three more bites of slack…about eighteen feet of line. I hoped they wouldn't ask questions when the weight left the line. I straightened up slightly and pulled out the Colt automatic.

The murmurings of soft voices reached me. I tried to judge the distance, but the sound bounced and echoed. I recognized Daisy's little voice, high-pitched and confused.

Finn hadn't heard me. I kept my mouth closed, forcing my breathing quiet. My heart hammered in my ears. Slowly I shuffled forward five feet, a third of the distance to the pump foundations.

In minutes Finn would return with Daisy. I knew I'd have the time and the strength for only one try.

# THIRTY-TWO

I EDGED MY way toward the old pump foundation. When I thought I was close, I reared up on my knees like an old dinosaur, hand outstretched and groping.

The edge of my hand touched cold, damp concrete. With infinite care I palmed the small automatic, held it against my chest, and pushed off the safety. I took a deep breath and braced my forearm on the concrete. The darkness in front of me was a solid door.

Finn would have to use the light to walk Daisy out. I strained to hear. Nothing.

"Keep your eyes on your feet, Ruth," he said. The voice took me completely by surprise. I crouched as low as my belly would allow. Their feet made soft shuffling sounds with an occasional tinkle as some small piece of mining detritus was kicked from their path.

The light cut the darkness over my head, darting out into the shaft. I kept my head down. My hand on the automatic was wet with sweat. The sounds stopped. Had the son of a bitch seen the rope?

"Gastner!" His voice was strong…and close. The beam of light twitched, swinging from one side to the other. "I've got the girl with me."

I could hear her breathing, little chirpy breaths of raw fright. He took another step, and I watched the flashlight beam.

His voice was a soft whisper. "Stay close, Ruth."

She wasn't linked. I gritted my teeth and slipped my index finger in the trigger guard of the Colt.

The flashlight beam was narrow and intense. He was close. Another step, you bastard, I thought. I saw the shadow of his hand behind the light, counted three, and moved.

Six feet away, the target for my automatic was just a murky figure behind the light. I saw Finn's trick almost soon enough. The images registered just as I squeezed the trigger. The smaller of the two figures was holding the flashlight.

I pulled the shot, but too late. The little Colt coughed and spat. The bullet sang past the side of Daisy's head, whined off the ceiling, and ricocheted down the drift.

Finn was already in motion, but he was a big target. I squeezed the trigger twice, and this time Finn yelped and spun sideways. In two staggering backward steps he crashed into the wall of the shaft.

Instinctively Daisy turned, and the beam turned with her. For a moment Finn was illuminated. He scrambled to his feet. In his right hand was my .45 automatic, and there was no silencer on the muzzle.

I pointed quickly and fired twice. Each time the little pellets struck him, he flinched and staggered back. But he didn't go down. For a moment he stood motionless, his face looking up at the roof of the drift, as if he were lost and searching for direction from the rocks.

The little girl dropped the light. It clattered, rolled a couple of feet toward me, and lay against a length of rusted pipe. Its beam pointed back into the drift. She whimpered and sat down, a tiny, frightened ball.

I slapped the automatic down on the concrete foundation, lunged toward her, and grabbed the harness. I pulled the little girl to me. I saw motion and looked up to see Finn staggering like a drunk. He raised the .45 and held it in both hands.

"Don't do it!" I shouted. Releasing my hold on Daisy, I made a wild grab at the little Colt. Finn swung toward me and pulled the trigger. The .45 bellowed, the explosion mind-numbing in the drift. The bullet passed harmlessly two feet over my head, crossed the main shaft, and thudded into a timber.

I locked my arm against the damp concrete, pointed the .380 toward the center of the shadow that was Finn's torso, and pulled the trigger twice.

Finn staggered backward. The drift was filled with the crashes of the .45 as his finger jerked the trigger spasmodically. I cringed low, hugging Daisy to me. One of the fat, hollow-point bullets of the .45 glanced off an iron bracket and sang over our heads like a wasp. Finn had already lost his balance, the recoil of the gun adding to his backward dance.

Another sound became harmony to the big automatic. With a loud "whump," a section of the wall just behind the timbers caved in, the mass striking Finn and carrying him to the other side of the drift. He screamed and went down. The dust billowed toward me.

I slapped the light switch on my helmet. In one desperate motion I stood up, pulled Daisy off her feet, and plunged the carabiner through the loop of my own harness. The spring snapped shut.

With the little girl hanging from my waist like a rag doll, I turned and waddled toward the vertical shaft.

Behind me, Finn screamed. "No! Listen to me!" he shrieked. The son of a bitch would have to talk to himself.

I fumbled with the mike switch on my collar. "Pull me up!" I bellowed into the mike.

Behind me, Finn continued to shriek and then he

found the .45 again. Its last cartridge exploded. The flash illuminated the back of the drift, and the slug danced off the rock and dug into the dust. Even as the clip emptied, the rumble of the earth's guts built, low and ominous.

A puff of air hit my face and with it came the acrid smell of fresh rock dust. A timber nearby cracked loudly and a shower of rocks clattered around my feet. I grabbed a fistful of Daisy's jacket and reached the mouth of the drift just as the last of the rope's slack snaked past. The rotten timbers above the pump station collapsed inward.

Something heavy struck my right foot and I spun sideways. "Son of a bitch!" I shouted and jumped into space.

The jolt of the rope damn near cut me in half. Daisy was a small child, but her weight pulled the harness off-sides.

Like a twisting, turning pendulum, we snapped out away from the drift and then crashed back against the side of the shaft, the iron of the ladder cracking my helmet. If Daisy screamed, I never heard it.

The rumble of the collapse died away in the drift even as we were lifted toward the surface. I hung limp, head back and eyes locked on the patch of light above me.

It was almost a relief to hang in the quiet shaft. "Gastner, you copy?"

In order to key the mike, I would have had to release my hold on Daisy. That would have been a hell of a way to test whether or not the carabiner still locked her harness to mine. I didn't have the strength to yell. Let 'em wait, I thought.

# THIRTY-THREE

A THOUSAND HANDS hoisted us out of the shaft. The ground under my feet was hard and firm—with nothing hanging over my head but the night sky.

"Be careful with the child," someone said. Her eyes were tightly closed, with her arms drawn up tightly to her chest and her fists balled under her chin.

I struggled to my feet and saw Nolan Parris. The priest was trying to reach the child, trying to push his way past the medical team and the assisting cops. His face was as white as his Roman collar and his eyes wide with concern for the child…but he was heading for disaster.

"Parris!" I shouted at him. He jerked up and saw me. I wrenched my arm away from someone and staggered toward the priest. I caught him by the shirtfront and for a minute we both executed a slow, clumsy dance as I tried to keep my balance.

I shook Parris until he was looking me in the eye.

"Listen!" I shouted at him and then I lowered my voice. "Listen to me. Now's not the time. You're a stranger to her, just like the rest of us."

"But I…"

I shook him, but it was a damn feeble shake. "Stay out of their way. She's in good hands. And you're not going to be able to just walk back into her life. She doesn't know you. You'll make matters worse." He turned in my grip and watched the medics bundle the little girl toward the medivac helicopter.

Hell, I knew what he wanted. He'd made up his mind and now wanted to make up for four lost years. But he had no idea how tough that road was going to be. The little girl wasn't going to run into his arms, shouting, "Daddy, Daddy!" I figured she'd had her fill of adults for a while. If I'd been her, I'd have wanted to stay catatonic for about a month until I sorted life out.

Camera lights bathed the helicopter as the reporters got what they had come for. A little, helpless, battered child made damn good copy.

I could see Nolan Parris wasn't going to do anything stupid, and I released my hold on him. "Help me over to the chopper. We'll ride into the hospital with her."

TWENTY HOURS LATER Pat Tate answered the telephone for me. I was standing in front of the small mirror that hung over the nightstand in my hospital room, trying to manipulate the electric shaver so I didn't hack my chin wattles to pieces. Even over the buzz of the razor, I heard the caller's ranting and knew right away who it was. "You betcha," Sheriff Tate said. He nodded and repeated himself, then added, "Here he is." He held out the receiver, and I set the razor down.

"Holman?"

"Himself."

Posadas County Sheriff Martin Holman was pissed. I got in the first word.

"Yup," I said into the phone and the tirade began.

"What the *hell* is going on up there with you?" he shouted, and I held the receiver away from my ear. Tate grinned, tapped his watch, and mouthed that he'd be

back in a few minutes. Holman was still barking, and
I let him roll on until he lost some momentum.

"My God, all I see in the papers and on television
is your mug, and for Christ's sakes you don't even
work for them."

"Those are the breaks," I said.

Holman almost choked, and I listened to him cough
for a minute before he got control. "Do you know how
many times I've called?"

"No, sir," I said. He was twenty years my junior,
but what the hell. He signed my paychecks. "No one
told me you'd called."

"Three times yesterday," Holman barked. He really
was angry. "Three goddamned times. And shit…four
times today, at least."

"Sorry about that. Things were hectic though." Pat
Tate must have been having fun. And the son of a gun
never had told me.

"They said you were asleep."

"The docs wouldn't let anyone in to see me. They
were worried about me combining exhaustion with
coronary stress."

"Coronary stress, hell. You've got the next best thing
to a new one. No one can kill you." His tone modulated
a little. "They could have at least told you I called."

"I'm sure they were planning on it." I saw an opening and took it. "And Estelle is doing well. I thought
you might like to hear that."

"I know that," Holman said. "I talked with her husband. More than once," he added pointedly. "He says
she's going to recover fully."

"Yes."

"So how the hell did you piece together that this

character was wanted in Washington? Talk about grandstanding heroics. Jesus."

"I didn't piece it together. He saw an old newspaper I'd kept after we got the APB earlier this month. He thought I had nailed him."

"You mean you hadn't made the connection?"

"Nope. I was as stupid as everyone else."

"Everyone is saying you did."

"Nope. Dumb luck."

"Well, I'll be damned. And he was in New Mexico when the murders took place in Washington...that's what Tate said earlier."

"That's right. He sent a friend back to Washington... a kid that lived with him. Slipped in, shot the governor and warden, slipped back out."

"Hell, he could as easily have ended up down here in Posadas, Bill. Right in our backyard."

"They have to end up somewhere. Pat Tate got lucky."

"And he was a nut case? That's what Tate said."

"In and out. We haven't had a chance to really sort everything out with the cops from Washington State, but from what they told us over the phone, Finn was treated at one of the state hospitals there about five years before. And he was treated as an outpatient on occasion before and after that. He and his younger sister used to run a fundamentalist church of sorts."

"He was a preacher?"

"Sort of. Fire-and-brimstone stuff. Eye for an eye. He was arrested once for assault, but that was tossed out. Apparently he managed to keep the lid on until his little sister was killed in a women's correctional facility a year ago."

"His sister?"

"Yes. A young woman named Ruth Tolever. She was arrested for something Finn contended she never did. She was killed during an altercation before she could be sprung on bail. The fight had nothing to do with her, they're telling us…she just got caught in it. That set Finn off. He blamed the whole system."

"He took his time, if revenge was what he had in mind."

"A planner," I said. "And the son of a bitch wasn't one of those nuts who wants to be caught. He moved down here, planning all the time what he was going to do. Hooked up with his young friend and found Arajanian was an apt pupil."

"And the little girl? The TV men sure had a field day with that story."

"As near as we can figure from what Washington tells us, Finn probably saw the little girl as a replacement for his sister…that's my guess. Maybe he really did love Cecilia Burgess. She was going to have his kid. Maybe he just kept her around so he could keep Daisy. We may never know for sure."

"One cold bastard." Holman fell silent for a minute. "He had his pal kill all those kids in the truck."

"That's the way it looks. The one kid lived, and from what he's told Pat Tate, that's what happened. Since revenge worked in Washington State he probably figured it'd work here, too."

Holman grunted. "So, how are you?"

"All right. Bruised and tired."

"When are you heading back?"

I chuckled. "By the end of the week, I guess. Not before. I want to stick around to make sure Estelle's on the mend and doesn't need anything. And they haven't brought my Blazer back yet either."

"My house burned down, you know."

"I know. Bob Torrez told me. Did you find the key to my place all right?"

"We're staying at the Essex Motel."

"For God's sakes, Martin, what for? Get the god-damned key and use my house."

Sheriff Pat Tate had stepped into the room. I grinned at him and looked heavenward. Holman said, "Well, I don't know…and it was arson. To cover up a robbery."

"No shit? Bob didn't say anything about that."

"Hell no. We didn't know until yesterday. I was going to tell you, but they'd never put me through to you. How could I?"

"What was taken?"

"The usual stuff. My stereo, some guns, pottery, a couple rugs. Stuff like that."

"Any leads?"

"None yet. I was kinda hoping you'd be back so I could go over some things with you."

"End of the week for sure. Any other messages?"

"No. Well, wait a minute." He shuffled papers. "Your daughter in Flint called. But she said it wasn't important. You're supposed to call her when you can. I think she saw something on television and got worried."

"Fine. Anything else?"

Holman laughed, his usual good mood returning. "I feel like I'm being dismissed."

"I didn't mean it that way," I said, although I had. "I got company, is all, and we got a meeting with about eight different law agencies from Washington…and the feds."

"Better you than me," Holman said. "End of the week, then. Give my best to Estelle and Francis. And tell Tate that you don't work for him."

"I'll do that." We hung up and I repeated Holman's message to Tate.

"By the time we're through with all the paperwork and all the meetings, you'll think that you do, kid," Tate said.

# THIRTY-FOUR

IT WAS GOOD to walk out of that hospital room. We took the elevator down one floor, then wound through enough hallways to disorient the most die-hard Boy Scout. The door of 467 was ajar.

Estelle Reyes-Guzman's bed was partially elevated. The bandages around her head, the white gown, and the white bedding made it look like her dark face was floating in a sea of cotton. Her hands were folded on her stomach and she looked peaceful.

Even as Pat and I started across toward the bed, she opened her eyes. It took her eyes a minute to adjust. She saw me and a slow grin spread across her face. Even in a hospital bed, stuck with tubes and wired to machines, she was lovely.

"Hey, sir," she said, and her voice was soft but clear. I took her right hand in my left. She looked at the new wad of bandages and sling that trussed my right shoulder and arm. "You're almost in one piece."

"Piece of cake," I said.

"You're going back to Posadas now?"

I shrugged. "Maybe by the end of the week. No hurry."

"You're going to keep house for Francis until you leave?"

I nodded. "I'm too cheap to pay for a motel, you

know that." She grinned again. "I'll stick around until you're out of this hole."

"This hole is costing the county about a grand a day," Tate said, but he wasn't complaining.

Estelle frowned and reached across with her left hand, patting the top of mine. "Have you seen Daisy?"

I took a deep breath. "No. But she's doing all right."

"She wasn't hurt?" I was sure Pat had told her the entire story, but she needed the reassurance.

"Just bruises. Physically, she's all right."

Estelle heard that correctly and her dark eyes searched mine. I shrugged. "It's going to be a long, maybe tough road for her, Estelle. We have no way of knowing what sort of crap Finn put in her head. Now she doesn't have anybody except Nolan Parris. He's decided to try for legal custody. And he wants to remain with the order."

"That'll never work," she whispered. Her grip on my hand tightened.

"Give him a chance. It might. There aren't too many other alternatives. Who knows? He might start a fashionable trend." She smiled faintly, closed her eyes, and released my hand. "She'll be fine, Estelle."

"Will you do me a favor?" she said without opening her eyes.

"Sure. Name it."

She turned her head slightly so that when she opened her eyes she was looking directly at me. "When you think she's ready, would you bring her up to see me?"

I hesitated, then nodded. "I'll see what I can do."

She visibly relaxed and looked at Pat Tate. "You take care of him, all right? Make sure he behaves himself."

Tate threw an exaggerated shrug and thrust his

hands in his pockets. "He's too old to learn anything, Estelle. You get yourself better and maybe he'll go home." He shrugged again. "That's our only chance."

We stepped out into the hall and damn near collided with Francis Guzman. The young physician looked like maybe he'd gotten an hour's sleep. "She's doing great, isn't she?"

"You bet," Tate said.

Francis turned to me. "You've got a key to the house?"

"Sure do."

He nodded. "See you for dinner then. Around six." He grinned and pushed open the door to Estelle's room.

"Around six," I said in mock disgust as we walked down the hall toward the elevator. "That's what they promised before all this started. And I'm still waiting."

\* \* \* \* \*

# REQUEST YOUR FREE BOOKS!
## 2 FREE NOVELS PLUS 2 FREE GIFTS!

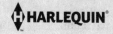

## ROMANTIC suspense

### *Sparked by danger, fueled by passion*

**YES!** Please send me 2 FREE Harlequin® Romantic Suspense novels and my 2 FREE gifts (gifts are worth about $10). After receiving them, if I don't wish to receive any more books, I can return the shipping statement marked "cancel." If I don't cancel, I will receive 4 brand-new novels every month and be billed just $4.74 per book in the U.S. or $5.24 per book in Canada. That's a savings of at least 14% off the cover price! It's quite a bargain! Shipping and handling is just 50¢ per book in the U.S. and 75¢ per book in Canada.* I understand that accepting the 2 free books and gifts places me under no obligation to buy anything. I can always return a shipment and cancel at any time. Even if I never buy another book, the two free books and gifts are mine to keep forever.

240/340 HDN F45N

Name _____ (PLEASE PRINT)

Address _____ Apt. #

City _____ State/Prov. _____ Zip/Postal Code

Signature (if under 18, a parent or guardian must sign)

Mail to the **Harlequin® Reader Service:**
**IN U.S.A.:** P.O. Box 1867, Buffalo, NY 14240-1867
**IN CANADA:** P.O. Box 609, Fort Erie, Ontario L2A 5X3

**Want to try two free books from another line?**
**Call 1-800-873-8635 or visit www.ReaderService.com.**

* Terms and prices subject to change without notice. Prices do not include applicable taxes. Sales tax applicable in N.Y. Canadian residents will be charged applicable taxes. Offer not valid in Quebec. This offer is limited to one order per household. Not valid for current subscribers to Harlequin Romantic Suspense books. All orders subject to credit approval. Credit or debit balances in a customer's account(s) may be offset by any other outstanding balance owed by or to the customer. Please allow 4 to 6 weeks for delivery. Offer available while quantities last.

**Your Privacy**—The Harlequin® Reader Service is committed to protecting your privacy. Our Privacy Policy is available online at www.ReaderService.com or upon request from the Harlequin Reader Service.

We make a portion of our mailing list available to reputable third parties that offer products we believe may interest you. If you prefer that we not exchange your name with third parties, or if you wish to clarify or modify your communication preferences, please visit us at www.ReaderService.com/consumerschoice or write to us at Harlequin Reader Service Preference Service, P.O. Box 9062, Buffalo, NY 14269. Include your complete name and address.

HRS13R

# REQUEST YOUR FREE BOOKS!
## 2 FREE NOVELS PLUS 2 FREE GIFTS!

**❤ HARLEQUIN®**

# INTRIGUE®

## BREATHTAKING ROMANTIC SUSPENSE

**YES!** Please send me 2 FREE Harlequin Intrigue® novels and my 2 FREE gifts (gifts are worth about $10). After receiving them, if I don't wish to receive any more books, I can return the shipping statement marked "cancel." If I don't cancel, I will receive 6 brand-new novels every month and be billed just $4.74 per book in the U.S. or $5.24 per book in Canada. That's a savings of at least 14% off the cover price! It's quite a bargain! Shipping and handling is just 50¢ per book in the U.S. and 75¢ per book in Canada.* I understand that accepting the 2 free books and gifts places me under no obligation to buy anything. I can always return a shipment and cancel at any time. Even if I never buy another book, the two free books and gifts are mine to keep forever.

182/382 HDN F42N

| | |
|---|---|
| Name | (PLEASE PRINT) |

| | |
|---|---|
| Address | Apt. # |

| | | |
|---|---|---|
| City | State/Prov. | Zip/Postal Code |

Signature (if under 18, a parent or guardian must sign)

Mail to the **Harlequin® Reader Service:**
**IN U.S.A.:** P.O. Box 1867, Buffalo, NY 14240-1867
**IN CANADA:** P.O. Box 609, Fort Erie, Ontario L2A 5X3

**Are you a subscriber to Harlequin Intrigue books
and want to receive the larger-print edition?
Call 1-800-873-8635 or visit www.ReaderService.com.**

* Terms and prices subject to change without notice. Prices do not include applicable taxes. Sales tax applicable in N.Y. Canadian residents will be charged applicable taxes. Offer not valid in Quebec. This offer is limited to one order per household. Not valid for current subscribers to Harlequin Intrigue books. All orders subject to credit approval. Credit or debit balances in a customer's account(s) may be offset by any other outstanding balance owed by or to the customer. Please allow 4 to 6 weeks for delivery. Offer available while quantities last.

**Your Privacy**—The Harlequin® Reader Service is committed to protecting your privacy. Our Privacy Policy is available online at www.ReaderService.com or upon request from the Harlequin Reader Service.

We make a portion of our mailing list available to reputable third parties that offer products we believe may interest you. If you prefer that we not exchange your name with third parties, or if you wish to clarify or modify your communication preferences, please visit us at www.ReaderService.com/consumerschoice or write to us at Harlequin Reader Service Preference Service, P.O. Box 9062, Buffalo, NY 14269. Include your complete name and address.

HI13R